ITALIAN RING CHARADE

CATHY WILLIAMS

Recycling programs for this product may not exist in your area.

ISBN-13: 978-1-335-61406-3

Italian Ring Charade

For questions and comments about the quality of this book, please contact us at CustomerService@Harlequin.com.

Harlequin Enterprises ULC
22 Adelaide St. West, 41st Floor
Toronto, Ontario M5H 4E3, Canada
www.Harlequin.com

HarperCollins Publishers
Macken House, 39/40 Mayor Street Upper,
Dublin 1, D01 C9W8, Ireland
www.HarperCollins.com

Printed in Lithuania

1 2 3 4 5 6 7 8 9 10 LIT 28 27 26 25

Jennifer was aware of Gabriel's presence behind her seconds before she felt the weight of his hand on her shoulder.

It rested there in a light caress. Then he leaned down and his breath was on her cheek as he dropped a light kiss on the side of her neck.

Her eyes widened. In passing, she noticed the way their audience was tickled pink by the caress. Mostly, though, she was too busy going bright red and trying to harness her scattered thoughts to do much but continue to redden.

"Good day, my darling?" Gabriel crooned. He straightened, pulled a chair right next to hers and sat. Their knees were touching. Glancing down, Jennifer felt her mouth go dry at the sight of his muscular thighs straining against the fine linen of his trousers.

She hurriedly lifted her gaze to the amused curve of his mouth and then to the dark eyes, shielded by impossibly long, sooty lashes.

"Already told you...er...darling...fabulous day."

When he squeezed her knee, then let his hand remain there, burning a hole through her summery dress, she licked her lips.

Cathy Williams can remember reading Harlequin books as a teenager, and now that she is writing them, she remains an avid fan. For her, there is nothing like creating romantic stories and engaging plots, and each and every book is a new adventure. Cathy lives in London, and her three daughters—Charlotte, Olivia and Emma—have always been, and continue to be, the greatest inspirations in her life.

Books by Cathy Williams

Harlequin Presents

The Housekeeper's Invitation to Italy
The Italian's Innocent Cinderella
Unveiled as the Italian's Bride
Bound by Her Baby Revelation
Emergency Engagement
Snowbound Then Pregnant
Her Boss's Proposition
Billionaire's Reunion Bargain
Heir for the Holidays
Maid for the Italian
Out-of-Office Temptation

Secrets of Billionaires' Secretaries

A Wedding Negotiation with Her Boss
Royally Promoted

Visit the Author Profile page
at Harlequin.com for more titles.

ITALIAN RING CHARADE

To my three fabulous daughters.

CHAPTER ONE

GABRIEL STOOD FOR a few moments and stared with a jaundiced expression at the heaving restaurant, if it could be called a restaurant, in front of him.

The Chick'n'Rib Shack.

He figured *shack* was more on the money than *restaurant*.

An impressive row of motorbikes was parked directly in front. Various groups of bikers were smoking and drinking by some of the bikes. A couple of interesting ladies in skimpy leather gear were sitting on the pavement, clutching bottles of beer and chatting.

The doors to the restaurant were flung open, pouring light and rock music out into the summer evening. The sun was shining and it was still hot, even though it was after eight in the evening. The place sat squatly in the middle of a parade of shops, two of which were boarded up and the other three closed.

As venues went, it hardly screamed *romance.*

On the plus side, the atmosphere felt jolly enough. He didn't expect any imminent fights.

On the minus side…*what on earth was she doing here*?

Gabriel pushed himself away from the black Range

Rover against which he had been leaning and strolled at a leisurely pace towards the restaurant, picking up sidelong, interested glances on the way.

He stood out.

Wherever he went, Gabriel Garcia stood out, and it wasn't simply because he was so strikingly good-looking. Yes, he was tall, exotically bronzed and stupidly physically beautiful, but there was also an aura of power and cool, quiet strength about him that made you want to stare at him—and then stare just a little bit more.

He was seldom aware of other people looking at him. Or if he was, he ignored it. He personally was never curious enough about anyone to stare at them.

Except now, he thought wryly, as he stood in the doorway of the restaurant, letting his gaze wander slowly through the crowd in search of her.

It seemed like a million people were crammed into the small space. Wooden tables were scattered in a random fashion in front of a stage where a DJ had set up camp and was throwing himself with gusto into his selection of rock classics. The naked brick walls were cluttered with posters of rock legends playing guitars or sitting with moody expressions on giant motorbikes.

A few tipsy women were dancing, and food was being ferried to tables where people were eating and trying hard to talk over the music and the laughter and the babble of raised voices.

He spotted her.

There she was, sitting with her back to him, her long, dark, curly hair tumbling halfway down her back, earnestly talking to the biker sitting opposite her. Even with her back to him, he would have recognised her from a mile away. Something about the straightness of her posture, the way she held her shoulders and crossed her ankles, tapping with her foot as if impatient for something to happen.

Gabriel didn't hesitate. He walked briskly towards the table, weaving his way through the crowd, and tapped on her shoulder without a second's thought as to whether she might be overjoyed to see him or not.

Of course she would be.

They were friends.

Some might say that she was his closest friend and he hers. In a world full of people impressed by his vast wealth and eager to do whatever he asked, she was a constant. She was the woman who had never been impressed by his money or status or…pretty much anything, for that matter.

They went back a long, long way. If, when the starting gun was fired, they were two people who came from two different worlds, then somehow that had never stood in the way of their friendship.

He straightened and waited for her to turn around.

Hell, who was she with?

Bulky guy…thick beard…several chunky chains…fascinating collection of tattoos on both arms…black vest…

Jennifer felt the tap on her shoulder and wasn't sure whether to be annoyed that someone was interrupting her date night or relieved because she didn't, actually, want to be on this particular date night and couldn't understand what had possessed her to swipe right when his photo had popped up.

Maybe she'd been feeling particularly adventurous at the time. Maybe she'd secretly been longing for a change from the sort of guys she was accustomed to dating, unadventurous teacher and accountant types who always seemed to be busy saving to buy a house while life and all its exciting possibilities rushed past them in a blur.

She was by no means a serial dater, but maybe she'd just opted for Hal the biker out of sheer frustration with her love life. How hard was it to find a soul mate? It wasn't as though she was one of those women in search of Mr Perfect, without whom life wouldn't be complete! She didn't have checklists. She didn't tick off good qualities, weigh them up against bad qualities and then come to an informed decision!

She was happy to go with the flow and see where things led. She was realistic! She knew that she wasn't perfect and neither were they, but love was about rising above imperfections and finding peace and harmony and fun and acceptance within an imperfect framework.

So where were all these perfectly imperfect guys? It felt like the ones she met only ever managed to make her yawn.

Including this one, despite appearances.

She turned round, and her eyes widened at the sight of Gabriel towering behind her.

Black polo shirt, black jeans…although his uniform of black looked nothing like the black ensemble her date, Hal, was wearing. As always, Gabriel looked effortlessly elegant and sinfully good-looking.

For a fleeting second, the punch of his raw sex appeal hit her for six before common sense quickly intervened, as it always did. This was Gabriel. Gabriel, who was so tightly woven into the tapestry of her life. Yes, he was sexy, but he was also forbidden fruit. It didn't mean that her heart didn't sometimes pick up pace when she saw him or heard his voice. She wasn't a statue, after all!

'Gabriel!' she shouted over the noise.

'Sorry to interrupt your hot date, Jen, but I have to talk to you.'

'What, *this very moment*?' The last person she'd expected to see when she'd turned round had been Gabriel.

She kept in touch with him all the time, but he'd only been to Sussex for a couple of flying visits over the past few weeks, and she hadn't been around for their usual meet-up.

'No time to hang around,' he had told her several times when they'd spoken on the phone.

'Business,' he had groaned only a few days before when he had called to catch up. *'I've spent more time out of the damn country than in it.'*

'I guess you could join us!' she bellowed now, half standing. Out of the corner of her eye, she could tell that her date was none too happy with the interruption while she, on the other hand, could not have been more relieved. Even though…

What on earth was Gabriel doing here?

She felt a sudden ball of dread in the pit of her stomach and stood up fully, frowning and looking at him with consternation.

He was six-foot-three, and she was almost as tall at five-foot-eleven. Tall and busty with rebellious long dark hair in need of a trim and bright blue eyes that came straight from her Irish mother. Blue eyes, dark hair, pale skin and freckles. Her height, on the other hand, was a direct gift from her father, who had been six-foot-four.

'Is it your mum?' she asked, pulling him towards her so that she didn't have to yell to be heard.

'You could say so.'

'What's happened? God, Gabriel, hang on. Let me get my bag.'

'Probably for the best. Impossible to have a proper conversation in this place.'

She turned to her date, who had also risen to his feet, and flashed him an apologetic smile.

'Sorry, Hal. Emergency.'

Hal was sulking. She could see it in his eyes. Despite appearances, he really was rather sweet. When he asked her whether he could get in touch, she was loath to be unkindly blunt, so she vaguely muttered something and nothing about *getting in touch...who knew what the future held...you're really nice...maybe I'm not in the right place for a relationship at the moment...but you're such a great guy...*

It was awkward having to half yell her feeble excuses, and she was acutely aware of Gabriel watching keenly from the sidelines.

Flustered, anxious and desperate to hear what Gabriel had to say, she couldn't wait to leave the too hot and too noisy bar. It was a blessed relief when they were out in the open.

'Okay, what are you doing here? How did you find me, anyway? Is everything okay with your mum? I've had my phone ringer on loud in case she needed to get in touch with me, not that I would have heard it, anyway.'

'I never pegged you for a rock chick, Jen. My car's

over there. We can go have a chat somewhere a little less hectic.'

'Just tell me what's going on. I can't stand the suspense.'

'How long have you been seeing the caveman?'

'That's a very unkind thing to say about Hal, Gabriel!'

'That depends entirely on whether you're interested in meeting someone who hunts for their food. Cavemen have their uses.'

She glanced at him, torn between telling him to mind his own business and knowing that saying that would be pointless because he would just say exactly what he wanted to say. It was the sort of relationship they'd had from the very first time she'd met him when she'd been nine and he'd been twelve.

She'd had to go with her mother during the long summer holidays to his house because the babysitter her mum used had decided to go to Europe for the holidays with her boyfriend, and she was too young to be left alone. Lizzy Carlton cleaned once a week for Gabriel's mother, who lived in an ancestral mansion on the outskirts of Arundel. The pay was great. She loved the house, loved his mother and would have chopped off her own arm before letting Francesca Garcia down.

Jennifer had been walking in the gardens with her sketch-pad, deciding what flowers to draw for a summer school project, when Gabriel had sneaked up from behind and pulled her hair. She'd spun round and whacked him. Hard. With her sketchbook.

He still mentioned that to this day.

He beeped open the Range Rover, and she hopped inside and slammed the door shut behind her.

'How did you know where I was?' she demanded, buckling up but then turning to look at him as he edged the car out of the space.

'I phoned your friend.'

'Which friend? I have lots.'

'The one with the cats.'

'Caroline. And you know that's her name, Gabriel. You've been to her house with me many times before.' Jennifer thought that her friend would have gone into a meltdown at the sound of Gabriel's voice on the phone. She harboured lustful thoughts about him even though she had a very nice boyfriend. She wasn't the only one of her friends who went a little fuzzy in the head whenever he was around. Jennifer got it. He was rich and gorgeous but…he was also the guy who'd never had a serious relationship in his life before and went through women with such speed that it made her head spin.

Sometimes she thought that her imperviousness to his charm and wealth and staggering good looks was what had kept their friendship so strong and steady. He might be as tempting as the finest of chocolate on a physical level, but on every other level…no. He was the guy who played the field with cheerful abandon, the guy who didn't believe in love. She was the girl who'd seen the love her parents had shared, had seen the way her mother had kept that love burning even when her dad had died all those years ago. She was the girl who wanted what her parents had had.

The things she and Gabriel found important in life were so very different.

Besides…if she'd ever got it into her head to have some sort of crazy crush on him…

Well, it didn't bear thinking about. He'd run a mile. Gabriel was allergic to commitment when it came to the opposite sex. She had no idea why and had never asked. Some questions remained out-of-bounds however strong a friendship, and that was one of them.

'So, you still haven't told me what's happening.'

'It's about my mother, but don't start worrying. She's fine.'

'Yes, she's been doing great since her heart op a month ago, but Gabriel…she still seems worried all the time. Mum goes across every day. Now she thinks that perhaps she ought to start staying overnight, just in case…'

'I don't think that's necessary.'

'Why do you sound weird when you say that?'

'That's your imagination playing tricks on you. Have you eaten?'

Momentarily distracted, Jennifer hesitated. Eaten? At the Chick'n'Rib Shack? Hadn't even been tempted.

'Thought not. Let's go have something to eat, and I'll do my best to explain why I've shown up out of the blue.'

'Maybe,' Jennifer mused, as he swung away from the brightly lit bar into the darkness of the honeycomb of streets, finally emerging on the outskirts of the town, 'having had cancer all those years ago, another bout of ill health has made her depressed, even though the consultant has said that she's doing really well?'

'I'm sure you're right,' Gabriel murmured, 'but let's not get lost in speculation.' She was aware that he slanted a sideways glance at her. She stared through the window with a small frown. 'I haven't seen you in weeks,' he continued. 'Tell me what you've been up to.'

'You know what I've been up to. You've been talking to me twice a week since the op so that I can tell you how things are going with your mum.'

'That's called you reporting back to me. Our phone calls have been brief, which was not of my choosing. Work. What can I say? It's ridiculous at the moment. Anyway, back to my mother. As you know, she has a habit of glossing things over when she tells me how she's doing. I need a variety of data so that I can get a realistic picture. On another note, I had no idea you were dating someone from a Hell's Angels gang.'

'I'm not *dating* Hal,' Jennifer said irritably. 'And he's not from a Hell's Angels gang. I'm not even sure Hell's Angels still exist!'

'Not dating? My mistake. I assumed you were when the cat friend told me that you were on a date, and then I found you with the caveman sharing drinks. Although it's not much of a date if he can't even run to buying you a meal.'

'You're impossible.'

'Have you missed me?'

He was grinning, but just for a second, *a split second*, Jennifer felt that something again, a twinge somewhere deep inside her. An unerring gut instinct told her it had to be firmly stifled.

'Nope.'

His grin widened.

'I'll take that as a yes.'

At this hour of the night, the traffic was light. They were at the local Italian restaurant within several minutes of leaving the Chick'n'Rib Shack.

He killed the engine, but instead of swinging open

his door, he leaned against it and looked at her in silence for a few seconds.

The atmosphere was suddenly charged. Or maybe, Jennifer thought, that was her imagination playing tricks on her because she was starving, and because her date with Hal had been a resounding disappointment.

'You're staring at me,' she said after a while. 'I'm shocked you don't know that that's rude.'

'I always miss your caustic sense of humour when I'm away from it for too long.' He grinned with lazy amusement. 'I have no idea what would have possessed you to date the caveman.'

'Stop calling him that!'

'Will you be seeing him again?'

'That's currently under review.'

'Say no more.'

'He's really nice,' Jennifer said a little too defensively.

'Not your type.'

'You have literally no idea what my type is, Gabriel.' She briefly wondered if *she* knew what her type was. If she did, then how was it that she was still in the dating game at the ripe old age of twenty-nine?

She decided that it was an advantage not to have a type. Having a type was very restricting. Gabriel had always had a type. Small, blonde and beautiful. She slanted a sideways look at him and shivered at the thought of him with a woman.

'Don't I? Actually, maybe I don't, but I'm guessing you'd go for someone intelligent,' Gabriel said thoughtfully.

'Hal happens to be very intelligent. He's a car mechanic. Just because he doesn't run around making billions like you, Gabriel, doesn't mean that he isn't smart.'

'Say the word and I could introduce you to any number of my friends.'

Jennifer burst out laughing.

She rested her hand on the button to open her door but looked at him for a few seconds with genuine amusement.

'I've met a few of your friends before, Gabriel,' she said dryly. 'They've always seemed to have small blonde things hanging on to their arms for dear life. A bit like you, if I'm honest. Not for me, I'm afraid.'

She was even more amused when Gabriel flushed. He so rarely allowed anything or anyone to get under his skin, but her remark had clearly hit home, and she wasn't going to apologise about that.

If he could make judgement calls on her love life, then she could make similar calls on his.

She usually kept her opinions to herself, aside from the occasional sarcastic comment, because his choice of women was his concern, but now and again a little prod didn't go amiss.

'Small blonde things can be fun,' he pointed out, recovering quickly and grinning right back at her. He reached across to open her door, and Jennifer tensed at the feel of his arm brushing her breasts.

She was suddenly hot and bothered—and annoyed with him for making her feel hot and bothered.

'I'm sure they can. Now, are we going to go have some food and actually get down to talking about what you interrupted my date to talk to me about? Or are we going to carry on sitting here, getting hotter and hotter by the second?'

When he burst out laughing, she went bright red. Belatedly she heard the double entendre in what she had just said.

'And you know I don't mean what...what you're cackling about!'

He was still chortling, though, as they made their way into the Italian restaurant, which they had both been to many times over the years.

She, of course, had been there a lot more often than Gabriel, because although she'd left to go to university three years after he had, she had returned to Sussex afterward. Whereas he had spread his wings and taken up residence in London before collecting places in New York, Hong Kong and Dubai like properties on a Monopoly board.

There had been no need for him to fly anywhere to earn a living because he came from money. His mother had lived in the same house forever, a vast ancestral country pile with acres of land.

He could easily have returned after university to run the estate, but instead he had got people in to do it, had sold off some of the acreage so that it was more manageable and had done his own thing.

He had concentrated on making his billions.

He had entered the lucrative world of property development, focusing on commercial property and specialising in warehouse space and land for out-of-town retail parks. Then, from that springboard, he had begun an inexorable process of eying up lucrative startups, buying them, investing in them and turning them into goldmines.

Without the need to initially think about financing what he wanted to do, he'd had the freedom to do whatever he wanted, to explore what made him money, safe in the knowledge that if he failed, he wouldn't end up sleeping under newspapers outside a shop.

He had gone exploring and had never returned to being the presence in her life she had become accustomed to over the years.

To his credit, though, he did come back to check in on his mother at very regular intervals. He was a devoted son.

She knew that the past few weeks had been rough for him because he hadn't physically been able to visit as much as he'd wanted, especially considering his mother's operation. But Jennifer knew that he'd kept in touch—not just with her for catch-ups, but over Zoom with his mum and with her consultant.

Which brought her back to the business of his mother and the mysterious reason he had suddenly appeared without warning earlier on.

She would wait until they were seated. She felt his hand on the small of her back as he ushered her ahead of him into the restaurant, which was packed to the rafters.

She had a flashing image of them together. He, so tall, so sinfully beautiful, dressed in the sort of uber-expensive label-free clothes that oozed sophistication, power and wealth.

While she, the very opposite of one of his tiny, Polly Pocket beautiful blonde little things, was in suitably appropriate gear for a date with a biker. Faded skinny jeans, flat lace-up ankle boots and a burgundy T-shirt that stretched over her abundant breasts. She'd resisted the temptation to complete the look with a bomber jacket, only because it was way too hot.

Jennifer privately felt that she had the sort of figure that very easily looked matronly if her clothes were too baggy, so she was happy to wear snug tops and damn the consequences.

Occasionally she wondered what Gabriel thought of her when they were together, whether he made mental comparisons to the petite blondes he was always out with, but she never lingered over those thoughts, never felt at all insecure, because they were so comfortable in one another's company.

'So…' she opened as soon as they were sitting. The waiter had somehow magicked up a table for them by the window that overlooked expansive gardens at the back.

'So…' Gabriel parroted. 'Does this mean that the pleasantries are over? There was something a little final about your tone of voice. Is it because you're annoyed that I interrupted your night of searing romance?'

Jennifer sighed elaborately and decided to ignore his shameless fishing for information. 'I guess I should be polite and ask you how you've been, but if you tell me that all you've been doing is working, then I'm going to yawn and talk about too much work and high blood pressure.'

'How is a guy supposed to run an empire and make money if he takes time off to go for country walks and put his feet up in front of a fire?'

'You don't have to work as hard as you do, Gabriel. In fact, you don't actually have to work at all. You never have.'

* * *

Gabriel didn't visibly react. He was accustomed to her gentle chiding when it came to his pressurised work life. It was a familiar backdrop to many of their conversations, and he knew that he would miss it if it ever disappeared, but for the first time, he really thought about what she'd just said.

Jen saw a lot of him and knew a lot about him. They shared a long history of friendship, but there were things even she didn't know and never would. Things he kept to himself. Secrets that only his mother could access.

Yes, there was the big house with the land and the family fortune.

But no one knew how that fortune had been ruthlessly depleted by his father, the man who had walked away from his own flesh and blood three decades ago, when Gabriel had been little more than a toddler.

To the outside world, it had been an amicable parting of ways. It was the story his kind-hearted mother had spun to everyone, including him. Retrospectively, he had realised that it had been to spare him the hurt of knowing just how comprehensively they had both been abandoned.

Gabriel had found out the bitter truth about the kind of man his father was when he was thirteen. But it was only after he had graduated from university, when he had begun to look, in detail, at financial records that went back over the years, that he'd discovered the full extent of what his father had done. His mother had reluctantly explained the divorce proceedings, and the picture painted had been of a bastard who had manipulated his devastated wife into handing over far more of her personal fortune than she had been legally obliged to. She had inherited her wealth from her parents, who had long since died, and had naively trusted the running of the estate to her husband. He, in turn, had squirrelled away money, and when he'd finally cut loose from them had successfully hidden vast assets in overseas accounts. He hadn't openly denied it to lawyers and had politely challenged them to find any such sums of money anywhere. They couldn't.

Gabriel had come from money, yes, but there was no way he could have ever sat back and enjoyed a life of doing nothing, even if he had wanted to.

He'd had to put his nose to the grindstone to make sure his mother was financially secure for the rest of her life, to make sure she didn't lose her family home, which was the only one she had ever known. His father had left great gaps in the savings and investments, and between theft, embezzlement and greed, what had been a fortune had been reduced to almost nothing.

His ability to work hard had come at a cost.

'Anyone there?'

Gabriel surfaced to find Jen reminding him of the waiter, who had sidled over to their table and was waiting for them to place their orders.

'Since when did you start daydreaming?' she teased. 'Wait, are you going to start turning into a real man?'

'Define *real man*,' Gabriel said absently. He glanced at the menu and ordered a complicated salad and a bottle of Italian red.

'Oh, the usual. Someone in touch with his feelings…expressive…knows how to talk about emotions…isn't ashamed to cry during a soppy romcom…' she said.

'Oh, yes, that sounds like exactly the sort of guy I'm turning into. How well you know me.' He sat back while red wine was poured for both of them and looked at her in silence for a few seconds.

She was so familiar to him and yet, right now, as he gazed at her with his head tilted to one side, he felt as though he was seeing her for the first time.

She might not be the sort he usually went for, because he invariably dated small, blonde, kittenish women who loved nothing more than to please him, but there was an intelligence about her and also…a strong, assertive attractiveness that was linked to that. In actual fact, she was really rather beautiful, with all that striking dark hair and dark eyebrows and those cornflower-blue eyes.

'Have your eyes always been that colour?' he suddenly asked, frowning.

'Sorry?'

'I don't seem to have noticed the colour of your eyes before. Unusual shade of blue.'

He continued to look at her as she reddened, temporarily flummoxed.

'Well, Gabriel, believe it or not, they've always been this shade of blue. Maybe you haven't noticed before because, if you recall, I used to wear glasses.'

'So you did.'

'Then I had laser treatment six months ago and hey, presto, no more glasses.'

'That explains it.'

'We still have to get down to why you've shown up out of the blue,' she pressed.

'I've decided to invest in a vineyard.'

'Sorry?'

'All my other business concerns are ticking over nicely, and I'm young enough to think about taking a few risks.'

Not at all what she had been expecting him to say. Jennifer frowned. Their gazes collided, and her tummy flipped at the thought of him noticing her eyes. The way he'd said that…not a throwaway compliment or a jokey, teasing observation. His voice had been a little bemused, as if he was seeing her for the first time instead of the millionth.

'Ah, I understand. That's where your mother comes in. You came to tell her first hand about this plan of yours, and then you decided to pay me a visit. Not exactly urgent enough for you to interrupt my date, though…'

'But you're not unhappy that I did,' he returned shrewdly.

'I suppose,' Jennifer admitted grudgingly. 'Hal wasn't going to get past the first post.'

'Thought not. You would have eaten him alive.'

'That's not very nice!' Jennifer objected, patches of colour staining her cheeks.

'It's actually meant to be a compliment, Jen, but moving on from that, that's only partially why I'm here.' He paused and shifted, and for the first time since he'd appeared from nowhere, he actually looked uncomfortable.

Jennifer was suddenly on red alert. Gabriel wasn't the sort of guy who ever looked uncomfortable. Even as a kid, he'd always had the air of someone who, at a push, could run the country.

She looked at him narrowly. Her heart sped up, and a thousand awful, frightening scenarios flashed through her head.

Was something wrong with him? Was he ill? Why a vineyard? Lord, what if he'd decided to permanently relocate to wherever this so-called vineyard was? What if he was going to completely disappear from her orbit? Selling up the family home and taking his mother with him?

She whitened.

'Have you actually put money down on this vineyard?' she quizzed sternly, diving into her glass of wine and gulping down so much that she nearly choked on the mouthful. 'There's such a thing as being rash! You're not a rash person! In fact, how many times have I told you that you need to be more spontaneous? But that's not who you are! Where is this place, anyway?'

'Italy, now that you ask, and Tuscany, to be more specific. Rolling hills…cypress trees…warm sunshine… rustic villages by the shedload… Have you ever been to Tuscany?'

'No,' Jennifer said shortly.

'Ever wanted to go?'

'Why do you ask?'

'Because I'm going in two days' time, and I'm asking you to come with me.'

'Sorry?'

'My mother will also be coming. I think it would do her good.'

'Gabriel, I'm not following you.' Jennifer was genuinely lost. She'd barely remembered what she'd ordered until it was now put in front of her. Calamari. He sat back as some kind of salad was placed in front of him, but then he immediately leaned towards her and looked at her with an intensity that instantly made her wary.

Mostly because she felt as though she was missing some kind of vital link in the conversation.

His eyes were intent and serious. Up close like this, she could see the flecks of gold in the dark, dark depths. His dad had been a strikingly handsome Italian, so her mother had once absently told her, and Gabriel had obviously inherited those looks.

She frowned and tried to join the dots.

'You're asking me to come with you?' Her frown deepened. 'To look at a vineyard?'

'I always welcome input,' Gabriel murmured. 'Although now that you mention it, I'll admit that isn't the only reason I'm asking.'

'Gabriel, I wish you'd just tell me what's going on. First of all, you show up without warning, tell me that there's nothing to worry about and that you're not here because of your mother except…you might be, and now you've decided that you want me to drop everything and head to a vineyard in Tuscany with you in a couple of days for no apparent reason. Can you get why I'm a little puzzled?'

Gabriel nodded.

He got it. Rarely was he at a loss as to what to say, but he was now, because he was about to wade into uncharted territory. He and Jennifer had a relationship that had grown over the years, had become firmly rooted in mutual respect and honesty. From kids through adolescence and into adulthood, with breaks in between when they weren't in the same place at the same time, they had settled into a rhythm that worked for them both.

The relationship was quite unlike any relationship he had ever had with another woman.

But now…he was about to introduce change, even if that change wasn't really going to alter anything.

He sighed and raked his fingers through his hair.

He pushed his plate to one side and looked at her carefully. In return, she pursed her lips in confusion.

'My mother's depressed,' he said flatly. 'She hasn't let on anything of the sort to me over the phone in the past couple of weeks, and I've spoken to her daily, as you know, but on the last call, she couldn't quite keep up the façade. You touched on it earlier. It seems that the combination of cancer all those years ago and now this situation with her heart…'

'Oh, Lord,' Jennifer said with a wince.

'She said she's staring mortality in the face, and she's scared.'

'But the consultant has said that everything is going great!'

'You and I both know that, but the mind…' Gabriel said drily, '…the mind can be irrational once fear takes hold, and that seems to be the case now. She's getting lost in thoughts of past regrets and, more importantly, things she feels she will die without achieving.'

'Like what?'

'Seeing me find myself a good woman and settle down.'

Jennifer didn't say anything, but personally, she thought his mother had a point. Would Gabriel ever find himself a good woman and settle down? He'd certainly never shown a single sign of doing any such thing in all the years she had known him. In fact, he'd always given the impression of being actively turned off by the idea.

She'd never asked him what, exactly, his problem was with commitment. She raised both eyebrows now and tried not to smirk.

'Well, you'd best start looking, then,' she advised tartly. 'I'm sure your pool of potential candidates is extensive. Might take you a few years to wade through it and narrow down your options.'

'I have no intention of doing anything of the sort, but it's important my mother doesn't lose sleep over this. With her recent heart problems, the last thing she needs is stress. And so here's where you come in.'

Jennifer was busily imagining what tiny blonde pocket rocket he might consider making his wife and quickly discovered that she didn't like the thought.

Was she so averse to the status quo between them changing? If so, then that was ridiculous. Everything in life changed over time. Certainly things would change between them anyway just as soon as she found herself a suitable partner! Gabriel might be a commitment-phobe when it came to women, but she had no such hang-ups when it came to men. If she hadn't found Mr Right yet, then she was looking in the wrong places.

She only surfaced to hear the back end of what he was saying. When it finally registered, her eyes widened, and she stared at him open-mouthed.

'A charade,' he was telling her smoothly. 'Just until my mother is back to her normal self.'

'Sorry…what?'

'She needs something to lift her spirits.'

'Okay, you've lost me.'

'How have I lost you? Have you been listening to a word of what I've just said?'

'My mind may have drifted.'

'How you manage to be such a great teacher is a mystery if you lose focus after five seconds.' He looked at her indulgently with fond amusement, but then the smile dropped, and he was utterly serious. 'My mother needs something to look forward to, Jen—and you and I? We could give her that. Together. Two people in love, in just the sort of relationship she wants for me. The two of us ready to settle down…'

CHAPTER TWO

JENNIFER'S JAW DROPPED. About to stick a piece of yummy calamari into her mouth, she paused and stared at him with incredulity.

She was still staring in gaping silence as he gently lifted the fork with the calamari out of her startled grasp and returned it to the bowl.

'You look like you might need to take a minute or two to digest what I just said. No problem. I'll just continue with the rabbit food on my plate until you regain your power of speech. By the way, I get it that you might be a little surprised at my solution.'

Jennifer finally found her voice. Her head was whirling. Yes, she'd heard what he'd just said, and yes, she knew from the expression on his face that he wasn't kidding, but she still feverishly wondered whether she had missed something in translation.

She looked at him narrowly.

'You're kidding, right?'

'You know I'm not, Jen.'

'How can you think that it would be a good idea to actually lie to your mother about something as big as this?'

'*Lie* is a very contentious word.'

'There's only one definition for *lie*, Gabriel, and it's

not telling the truth. You want me to agree to lie to your mother, who is someone I *love*!'

'But look at it this way…it would be for the greater good.'

Jennifer returned to the calamari, but her appetite had disappeared, and her thoughts were all over the place.

Suddenly, the easy course of their friendship seemed to have nosedived into unknown territory. Compared to Gabriel, she knew that she was very straightforward. No broken family background to deal with, although millions of children were the products of a divorce. Until her father had died, her parents had been blissfully happy.

She wanted the uncomplicated things in life—a man she loved who loved her right back, marriage, kids. No drama, no chaos, no ups and downs. She might not have found the right guy just yet, but she would get there. She wasn't riven with doubts about what she was looking for or eaten up with pointless worries about whether she would ever find him. She knew she would.

Gabriel, with his chequered love life, his disinterest in settling down, his crazy prioritising of work, represented a lifestyle she could roll her eyes at, whilst also disapproving of it—insofar as it went against everything she held dear.

But she loved him as a friend. She knew him and she never judged him, because none of his choices had ever affected her personally.

But now? There was the distinct whiff of danger, of lines being crossed. Pretend to a relationship that didn't exist? Everything inside her fought against that idea because it was so much the polar opposite of the kind of relationship she craved. It would feel like a travesty.

No way.

'For the greater good? That's a stupid reason,' she said flatly. 'Anyway, it doesn't matter what you say, I'm not going to lie to your mother about us and pretend that we're some kind of item.' She glowered and carried on with her calamari. He nabbed a piece from her plate but continued to look at her in silence.

'She's really not in a good place, Jen.'

'I know what you're trying to do, Gabriel. You're trying to guilt-trip me into going along with some insane idea that wouldn't work in a million years.'

'Of course it'll work.'

'Look, I understand that you're worried about your mother. We're all worried about her! And I also understand that she might be in an anxious place, keen to see you happily settled with someone before she…goes, *which she won't be doing for Heaven's sake*, but your idea is preposterous.'

'Is it really?'

'If you're that desperate to convince your mum that you've suddenly become the guy who can't wait to settle down, then good luck to you. Like I said, you can head straight to your little black book and get one of your many women to fill the role.'

'That's not going to work.'

'Why not?'

'Because I have no intention of settling down, and if I get in touch with anyone else, I run the risk of them…' He hesitated, and Jennifer raised both eyebrows.

'Ah…say no more, Gabriel. I get the picture.'

Gabriel raked his fingers through his dark hair and flushed.

'I'll rescue you from your discomfort, shall I? You run the risk of whoever is on board with your scheme actually thinking that it's the real deal, that you might actually put a ring on her finger and start planning a big white wedding. I already feel sorry for the poor woman.'

'Big white weddings aren't my thing, as you know. Nor are little off-white ones. I'm allergic to the thought of any weddings at all, actually.' Gabriel scowled. Jennifer looked at him calmly and continued eating her calamari, which had now gone tepid. She gave up and pushed the plate to one side, folding her hands on the table.

'Have you thought,' she mused, 'that you might actually use this opportunity to really think about settling down? I mean, I'm sure your mother wouldn't expect you to produce a fiancée from thin air like a rabbit from a hat, but she would be so happy if you simply told her that you intended to finally settle down.'

Deafening silence greeted this.

'Then there would be no having to lie, no having to pretend anything.'

Gabriel met Jennifer's bright blue eyes in stony silence. She was the only woman on earth who would ever be allowed to ask him that question, serene in the knowledge that he wasn't going to completely shut her down and sever the relationship forever.

Intensely private when it came to anything personal, Gabriel thought, just for a second, about a past he had never been able to escape and the way it had dictated the course of his entire future.

His father walking out on him and his mother had been the start of a long journey towards the disillusionment that had sealed him off from the possibility of ever taking a chance on love.

His mother had loved her husband. The small, beautiful, blonde English rose had been infatuated with the tall, dark, handsome Italian. Gabriel had gleaned that over the years, seeing the faraway look in her eyes whenever his name had been mentioned.

She'd lost her heart to a guy who'd turned out to be a complete bastard, and she'd never quite managed to get that heart of hers back, which was probably why she'd never had another man in her life.

He'd been aware she was hiding something, which was why, at the age of thirteen, Gabriel had bunked off school and taken a train to visit his father. If he was the good guy his mum never complained about, wouldn't he want to see his son? The need to find out had been overwhelming. His mother's silence had left a void that had demanded filling.

Finding out where Vincenzo Garcia lived had been a case of ingenuity and downright breaking and entering. He had fiddled with the lock on one of the drawers in the study his mother used for her admin. There, at the bottom of a stack of paperwork, he had found the divorce papers and the address where his father lived.

Would he still be there?

Gabriel hadn't given that a passing thought. He had worked out the trains and gone to his dad's house when he should have been at school. There he had found a half brother two years older than he was, who had been at home studying for exams and had barely raised his head to look at him, and a father who had been coldly unwelcoming. *'Didn't she tell you?'* he had asked with malice.

'Still playing the saint, is she? You upper-class English people with your stiff upper lips. No wonder I couldn't stick it out with your cold-as-ice mother.'

And there the conversation had ended.

Why had he gone?

It was a question he had asked himself over the years. Because he had carried the weight of guilt that he, as a toddler, had somehow been responsible for the break-up of their marriage? Or had he wanted to find out if, after all those years, there might have been a father/son bond there waiting to be explored?

He had returned home to a desperately worried mother, but had kept his visit to Vincenzo and his second family a secret.

And then, several years later, the truth about the wrecked finances had emerged. A man who had married for money and then betrayed his wife in the worst possible way.

Love, for Gabriel, resided in a place where only pain was the eventual outcome.

Love, marriage and pointless fairy tales about happy-ever-afters were for other people. Not for him.

He would never allow himself to be vulnerable enough to be hurt by anyone.

Jennifer was sucked into the dragging silence as she watched him disappear into a place where she couldn't follow, and for the first time, she knew that she had been locked out.

'Okay,' she said as the silence continued to stretch between them with an electric charge that brought her out in goose bumps. 'I get it. No to the settling down.' She shrugged. 'I still won't be taking part in any charade, Gabriel. I'm sorry to let you down, but I just…couldn't do that to your mother.' She didn't add how, in some weird way, she would have felt as though she might be betraying her own principles, her own *dreams*, by claiming a love that wasn't real.

For a couple of seconds, Jennifer wondered whether he was hearing her at all or whether he was still lost in the place to which he had retreated.

A place whose existence she had known nothing about. Hard on the heels of that realisation came something else—a stirring curiosity to find out what had commandeered his attention to the point where he had completely shut her out.

She knew so much about him.

She'd always smugly thought she knew *everything*. She was the one woman in his life who occupied a special place because she knew him much more deeply than any of the women he'd dated who flitted in and out of his life, never staying long enough to make a mark.

On a platonic level, she was his soulmate.

Except, she thought now, was she? Really?

'I should be heading back,' she said abruptly.

'Why?' he asked, suddenly snapping out of his introspection.

'Because I have lots of things to do.'

'Interesting. Such as what?'

'Such as recovering from my date with Hal.' She smiled, keen to get away from the suddenly alien place in which she had found herself, a place where her relationship with Gabriel had taken on a different and confusing dimension.

'Yes, I understand that that might have been a disturbing experience. But I thought you said that he was one of the smartest guys you'd ever met?'

Jennifer laughed and followed suit as Gabriel stood up, nodding to a passing server and tapping his phone to pay without bothering to look at the bill.

He really was stupidly sexy, she absently thought. Tall, dark and handsome to the ultimate degree. No wonder women flung themselves at him.

How on earth he could ever have imagined his mother would have bought into the fiction that they were an item was a mystery. She just wasn't his type physically, and men always went for a type.

'Here's why it wouldn't have worked anyway,' Jennifer mused aloud as they headed back towards his car.

'Are we off the topic of the caveman?'

Jennifer ignored the question and slipped into the passenger seat, waiting until he slammed the door after her. When he was behind the wheel, she turned to him as she fastened the seat belt.

'Look at the kind of women you go out with, Gabriel.'

'Rapid change of topic. Okay. Let's see where you're going with this.'

'I mean, you date tiny little blonde things who think you're the greatest thing since sliced bread.'

'Now I'm hurt.' But he was grinning as he started the engine and began pulling away. 'You mean *you* don't think I'm the greatest thing since sliced bread?'

'So your mother,' Jennifer continued, again ignoring his interruption, 'would never in a million years fall for some tall tale about the two of us...what? Suddenly discovering that we're a match made in Heaven?'

'Why not? People believe what they want to believe. And honestly, in many ways, we *are* a match made in Heaven.'

Except, Jennifer suddenly thought, *for those bits of you I know nothing about...those bits of you I've only just glimpsed...except for the fact that I believe in love and marriage, and you don't...*

'I can't say Mum has ever approved of any of my girlfriends,' Gabriel admitted as he began driving off.

'That's because you only give them five minutes before you get bored and move on to newer models. How could she ever actually get to know any of them in any depth? Where are we going, by the way? Are you dropping me home?'

'Back to mine. I bought you a present.'

'Will your mother be up?'

'Doubtful.'

'What present? You can give it to me another time, can't you? How long will you be staying?'

'Long enough, and I could, but I want more time to try and persuade you to see my point of view and climb on board with my plan.'

'That's never going to happen, Gabriel.'

'I dislike the word *never*. And speaking of types, why do you think that I'm only capable of going for one particular type of woman?'

'I can't recall ever seeing you with any woman who wasn't small and blonde and adoring.'

With a start, Jennifer realised that despite their long, long friendship—a friendship that had covered so many things, a friendship filled with laughter, heated debates and downright teeth-clenching arguments—despite all of that, this was the very first time they were touching on a subject that they had both mutually shied away from.

They had never seriously discussed each other's love lives in any depth.

'I like women to be soothing additions to my life,' Gabriel explained now. 'I'm not unusual in that. A lot of men in high-pressure jobs can't face a shrew on the home front.'

'That a very polarised view. Why does the opposite of an undemanding plastic doll have to be a nagging shrew riding on a broomstick? Can I say that I'm disappointed in you?' Her voice was light, but somewhere inside she really *was* a little disappointed. Did he really mean that? 'What about someone who challenges you intellectually?'

'I deal with enough intellectual challenges on a daily basis. Besides, if I want a woman to intellectually challenge me, I always have you.'

'That's another reason your mother would burst out laughing if we were to produce this piece of fiction out of thin air. She knows you like docile women, and we argue all the time.'

'Not all the time, and I wouldn't say we ever really argue.'

'You always have a point of view on the guys I go out with.' Jennifer sniffed. 'And it's hardly ever flattering.' But those weren't arguments. He teased her just like she teased him, and they always kept it superficial.

Until now.

They were approaching Gabriel's home, which was set amid countless acres of gently undulating open land with spectacular views of the South Downs.

Jennifer never failed to be impressed by the size and elegance of the estate every single time she approached the family mansion along a long, tree-lined drive bordered with towering ancient oak trees and open fields.

It revealed itself slowly.

In the fading summer light, the vast, stately Georgian manor house was always so impressive with its honey-coloured stone and the banks and banks of sash windows. Creeping ivy clad the south-facing walls, and the entrance was through a porticoed, sheltered outer area where wellies and brollies were dumped on wet, cold days.

Behind the house there were formal gardens and an orchard and various stables, once used but not anymore.

The car swung round the courtyard, and he stopped just by the fountain.

'Gabriel, how will I get back to my house? I mean, I could walk…'

She shared a small three-bedroom bungalow on the outskirts of the town. It was *her* family home, and she still lived there with her mother while she saved for a deposit on a place of her own.

'I have no idea why you won't let me buy you somewhere to live, Jen.'

This was a familiar bone of contention between them.

'You know why.'

'Remember the saying that pride comes before a fall?' Gabriel levered himself out of the car and swung round to open the passenger door before she could get to it. 'There's another way to consider what we discussed at the restaurant,' he said in a thoughtful undertone, standing close to her so that she was obliged to stare up at him.

Jennifer could breathe him in. The backdrop of his family home, silhouetted against the open land like a proud, impressive matriarch, framed him, and he looked truly like the lord of the manor.

She blinked away the oddest feeling that a part of her was seeing him for the very first time.

'Really?' She raised her eyebrows and folded her arms.

'Really.' He turned away and began moving towards the door, fishing in his pocket for the solid front door key but leaning into her alongside him so that his voice remained low and husky and persuasive.

'You could look at it as a job, of sorts.'

Jennifer stopped dead in her tracks and stared at him.

'A job? You mean a sort of holiday job because I have the summer off from teaching? Somewhat like extra out-of-school tuition for one of my pupils, but with slightly different ground rules?'

'I'm ignoring the sarcasm. You can frame it any way you like, Jen, but think about it for a minute. For the sake of a couple of months of doing what I know would really help my mother emerge from the doldrums that threaten to consume her, you would be paid. Like any job. Magnificently. You would be able to buy yourself the house you've been saving to buy for the past fifty years.'

'That's really coming at it from a different angle.'

'Damn it, Jennifer!'

Their eyes collided, fathomless black clashing with cornflower blue. Jennifer shivered, because there was nothing amused or light-hearted or indulgent in his dark, angry, frustrated gaze.

'You're not listening to me,' he grated. 'You've decided to occupy the moral high ground. Believe me, I wish I could think of some other solution to help my mother. But when she cried on the phone to me, it was the first time I'd ever heard her cry.'

'Gabriel…'

'No! Just listen to me for a couple of minutes, Jennifer, because this is bigger than you perhaps think.' He shook his head and raked his fingers through his hair. Then he stared down at her narrowly. 'After my mother called, depressed and tearful, I contacted her consultant. He said that stress, at this stage of her recuperation, is the one unknown that can send her hurtling in the wrong direction.'

'What do you mean, *hurtling in the wrong direction*?'

'Another and more significant stroke. Something from which she might never fully recover. So, yes, I get that I've thrown you a curve ball, but you need to really think about it.'

'Lying always ends up being so complicated.'

'You've had much experience of this sort of thing before?'

'No, but…'

'Right. You haven't. You teach, and for you there is clear blue water between what you consider right and what you consider wrong, except there are times where there's no such thing as clear blue water.'

Jennifer turned away and began walking towards the front door, this time confused and thoughtful.

Was she that inflexible? She liked to think of herself as liberal and open-minded, but somehow he had made her seem rigid in her thinking. How could he understand those blurry feelings inside her? He had no idea how rooted she was in the purity of love. For him, this was something she could do, something as a friend and as someone who cared deeply for his mother, so why wouldn't she do it?

Deep down she wondered if that was what he really thought of her. As someone who didn't quite know how to bend with the wind. Was that who she was? Someone in pursuit of the ideal to the point where her vision was blinkered? She was uncomfortable with that thought.

Had they just been skimming the surface of a friendship for all these years, or was this new terrain because another dimension had been introduced? A personal dimension, not between friends, but between a man and a woman.

Her heart picked up pace, but her thoughts remained muddled. She watched as he inserted the key into the lock.

He looked at her and said, seriously, 'My mother would love it,' his deep voice rising in his driving need to just *make her listen to what he was trying to say.* 'It would make her incredibly happy for her to know that you and I are on the road to getting engaged, that we're in a serious relationship.'

And just as Jennifer was on the verge of asking the ridiculously obvious question…*but then what happens when she finds out that it was all a sham?*...the door was pulled open and there was Francesca Garcia, her thin, aristocratic face haggard and tired, but still incredibly beautiful and wearing a smile that stretched from ear to ear.

'Yes, she would!'

Jennifer gaped, mentally wrestling with what Francesca had just said, appalled as the significance of it hit her like a blow.

She stared at the woman she considered a second mother.

Francesca Garcia was slender and willowy. Once blond, her hair was now threaded with silver but still long and pulled back into a bun at the nape of her neck. She had green eyes and the sort of soft, cut-glass accent so indicative of the English upper echelons.

Everything about her was gentle and elegant, from the string of pearls that never left her neck to the discreet Cartier watch that never left her wrist.

'Darlings, I happened to glance out of my window, and I saw the two of you outside in the car. I thought I'd come down and greet you myself. Come in, come in! Jennifer, my darling…'

There were tears of joy in her eyes, much to Jennifer's growing consternation.

She could feel Gabriel's brooding presence just behind her. She could recall the intense urgency of his voice when he had told her just how happy his mother would be to know that they were an item, that they werc on the way to becoming engaged to be married.

He had meant that statement to be one of desperate persuasion, spoken in an earnest, last-ditch attempt to bring her round to his impassioned point of view.

Jennifer knew that his mother had heard something quite different. She had heard a declaration of intent, of a relationship only waiting to be sealed.

They were both being hurried in, and the imposing door shut behind them.

From nowhere, George, the handyman who ran the gardening crew and the cleaning staff, appeared and smiled.

'Something to drink, sir? Miss Carlton?'

Francesca smiled and tapped him lightly on his arm. 'There's no earthly reason for you to be up and about and offering us drinks, George. You go straight back to bed and leave these treasures to me.'

'I… I hadn't planned on staying, Francesca.' Jennifer still hadn't looked in Gabriel's direction. She wondered whether she could somehow dodge the inevitable bullet by making a quick exit, but no such luck. They were both being trooped through into the smallest of the sitting rooms, and then…

'Darlings! I can't believe that you two are going to get engaged! Naughty Gabriel, keeping that under your hat! I can't tell you how excited I am by this news. Jennifer, my love, I expect Gabriel told you…' Francesca's eyes filled with tears. 'It's been so hard, frightening. There were times when I wondered what the point of anything was, felt like my life was over, so eventful, so filled with joy and sadness, and yet I couldn't help but think that I would die with nothing to show for it. But now… I can't believe my ears, my darlings! When? How? I always knew that you two would one day see sense and end up together.'

Jennifer finally looked at Gabriel, who stared back at her intently with his head tilted to one side.

She knew what he was thinking. She'd been so adamant that she would have nothing to do with a charade that might lift his mother from her gloom that he was now leaving it up to her to deny everything.

She opened her mouth just as Francesca reached out to clasp both her hands in hers.

'It's late,' Francesca said. 'You're tired. We can talk about this in the morning. Jennifer, please do stay the night. Then we can be up early, walk through the rose gardens. I know how much you love them. I'm so thrilled!'

'I've got to get back home, Francesca. You know how my mum is. She's expecting me…'

'Does she know?'

Jennifer glanced at Gabriel, who stared right back at her in lazy, amused silence.

'Know what?' she hedged.

'That you two are thinking about getting engaged, of course, darling! At long last.'

'It's not… We're not…' Jennifer heard her own voice, feeble and weakly protesting. 'There's a lot to think about… I mean…'

She felt Gabriel's arm as he slung it over her shoulder. For a few seconds, she froze, and all her jumbled thoughts left her head. The weight of his arm felt intimate…pulled her into a place never explored before.

'It's a big step, Mum,' he murmured, 'and of course it's not something we've discussed with anyone else. Yet…'

Francesca made a zipping motion with her finger across her mouth, but she was still beaming like the cat that got the cream.

'Understood,' she said with a girlish laugh. 'I shall

head up to bed, my darlings, but you can't imagine how happy you've made me.' She moved and pulled them both into a warm hug. 'I've been in a dark place, but now I see light. How I love you both…'

CHAPTER THREE

'BEFORE YOU SAY a word—' Gabriel was the first to break the frozen silence '—life is full of unexpected developments, and that was one of them. I did *not* see that coming. Drink? Let's decamp to the kitchen.'

'Unexpected developments? Drink? Kitchen? Gabriel, this is a nightmare!'

Jennifer looked at him with appalled eyes. In the space of half an hour, life as she knew it had been turned on its head. He was lounging against the wall, cool as a cucumber and if not whistling a merry tune, then certainly not looking as though the sky had fallen.

Which, she thought furiously, it hadn't. Not as far as he was concerned. He'd sought her out with a mission to woo her into agreeing with his harebrained scheme to pretend they had a relationship. Now, despite the fact that she had dug her heels in and adamantly refused to do any such thing, he would be thinking that Fate had stepped in at just the right moment and lent him a helping hand.

She decided she needed a drink after all.

'Gabriel,' she hissed, falling in alongside him as he headed towards the kitchen, 'you're going to put this right. I mean that!'

She sneaked a sideways glance at him and sighed with frustration.

'I mean it, Gabriel. I know you didn't plan on your mother overhearing our conversation and jumping to all the wrong conclusions, but this is *your* mess, and *you're* going to have to deal with it.'

'You could have said something back there, Jen. Why didn't you?'

'That's not the point.'

'You didn't because you could see how happy my mother was, how much her spirits were lifted, and you couldn't bring yourself to be the one to break her heart. No one wants to be the bearer of bad news, but after spending the past hour telling me that there was no way you could bring yourself to tell a few white lies for the sake of my mother's mental and physical well-being, you had the perfect opportunity to derail her hopes at the source.'

'A few white lies?'

'What would you like to drink? Tea? Coffee? Wine? Spirits?'

'It's late.'

'Not that late.'

They were in the kitchen. It was a wonderful space, huge with flagstone floors and a four-oven AGA in deep British racing green. Over the years, Gabriel had made sure that much of the vast manor was updated, with no expense spared. Pale wood and marble had gradually replaced ageing tiles and worn woodwork. Dated wallpaper had been stripped off walls and given way to a canvas of muted creams and pale pastel shades. Old paintings which had been in the family for decades remained but alongside them, a collection of modern masterpieces had slowly been built up over the years.

Only the kitchen remained as it always had been, because Francesca had refused to have it ripped out and modernised.

A central island dominated the space in the middle. To one end, a sturdy oak table stretched almost the width of the room. She could remember occasionally sitting here way back when, doing her homework, with Gabriel opposite her and her mother somewhere in the bowels of the mansion, cleaning.

Beyond the table, a sprawling, comfortable conservatory overlooked the acres of fields with a distant view of the castle just about visible beyond the stretches of land.

'I suppose I'll have a glass of wine,' Jennifer huffed. She went to sit on the comfy patterned sofa in the conservatory and thought about what he'd said.

Yes, she could have told Francesca that there had been a misunderstanding, that there was no engagement. She? Gabriel? Engaged? She could have laughed the whole thing off, but Gabriel was right.

She hadn't done that because she'd seen just how happy Francesca had been, and in a flash had also seen just how unhappy and fragile she'd been during the weeks of her recuperation. It was like realising just how awful the *before* shot was as soon as you saw the *after* one.

She'd thought Francesca had been doing just fine because the consultant had said that physically, at least, she was on the mend and doing very well. She hadn't looked beyond that to the older woman's mental state, which had been doing, she could see now, a lot less fine.

Discomforted, Jennifer looked at Gabriel warily from under her lashes as he sat next to her on the sofa holding two glasses of wine, handing her one.

'She was putting on a brave face,' Gabriel said flatly, 'until she could no longer do it and everything came pouring out. You've seen the remarkable turnaround this evening when she overheard our conversation. She's now a woman with a new lease on life.'

'You should have just got in touch with me. We could have had a nice, friendly, adult conversation about the situation instead of jumping in at the deep end and coming up with your own crazy solution to the problem.'

'I've always been solution-oriented. Tell me, what would have been *your* nice, friendly, adult conversation about the situation?'

Jennifer gave it some thought. 'Therapy.'

'Therapy?'

'Don't be such a dinosaur, Gabriel.'

'Tell me how you see a couple of sessions with a shrink doing the job.'

'She would have realised that there are reasons for being happy, for being grateful that she's recovering so wonderfully well. She would have seen that she didn't have to rely on her workaholic son finding a mate and settling down to give her a purpose for living.'

Gabriel looked at her with a pensive expression. 'Isn't it a natural desire for a parent to see her one and only child settled? You're an only child as well. I'll bet your mother can't wait to see her daughter married off to a nice young man who bears no resemblance to all the losers she's spent the past few years dating and getting rid of because they didn't live up to expectation.'

'Don't make this about me! And I don't date *losers*, Gabriel Garcia!' She swallowed half the glass of wine in one gulp and nearly choked.

'It'll work, Jen. It'll get my mother out of the doldrums and give her something to look forward to. No well-intentioned therapist would be able to do that. If not believing in all that kumbaya nonsense makes me a dinosaur, then I'm a dinosaur. To the best of my knowledge, my mother is of the same opinion. Don't forget the generation she comes from and the type of woman she's always been. Proud and self-contained. I don't see her pouring her soul out and weeping on a therapist's couch, do you?'

Put like that, Jennifer had to grudgingly agree with him. Francesca *was* a proud and self-contained woman. 'And then what happens once your mother's out of the doldrums?' She arched her eyebrows and looked at him steadily. 'Do we then break it to her that it was all a big fat lie?'

'That's a very dramatic way of putting it. We very carefully break it to her that we've discovered we make better friends than we do lovers.'

The breath caught in Jennifer's throat. *Lovers?* It was something she couldn't get her head round, but all at once that disturbing notion was planted. Her mind was suddenly unleashed and roaming free into all sorts of crazy alien territory.

Forbidden territory, because on any level other than the friendship one, Gabriel Garcia was not her type.

'Easy as that, is it?' Yet Jennifer's voice was tart as she tried to conceal the jump in her nervous system and the dangerous disobedience of her thoughts.

'Very easy.'

'Why are men so simplistic?' she scoffed with dripping sarcasm.

'Are you casting your mind back to the biker I rescued you from? I'm being serious, Jen. It would be easy for my mother to understand that in the end we couldn't take our very deep friendship to the next level. It would also make her realise that the mere fact that I contemplated settling down with you was an indication I'm finally in the right place. I'm finally realising it's time for the next chapter in my life.'

'You're so clever with words, and I'm not saying that as a good thing.'

'I'll still take it as a compliment.' He flashed her a winning grin, but then his expression turned serious. 'She'll be in a much happier place,' he said with genuine feeling. 'That's the most important thing. I don't want to think that every day brings the possibility of my mother entering a depressed world from which she might not return, and I know you love her. I know you wouldn't wish that on her either.'

'I feel I'm being railroaded into doing something that goes against all my principles.' And oh, how she did. His proposition sounded so simple, and yet it stuck in her throat because it somehow made a mockery of the very real relationship she'd spent a lifetime craving.

But how happy Francesca had looked…wasn't that worth everything?

'I know.'

His voice was low and serious as he reached out and covered her hand with his and squeezed it.

Gabriel could see the concern on her face and knew that he was putting her in a difficult position, but surely she could see where he was coming from? That there were times when only the bigger picture mattered, and this was one of those times? When a small sacrifice was worth the greater gain?

'Life's not black and white, Jen. Trust me, this is a harmless piece of fiction for us that could make an enormous difference to my mother.' He frowned thoughtfully. 'And now that I think about it, it's possible I really might be getting to a place where I'm willing to indulge the prospect of settling down. Maybe my mother's open desire to see me married has made me seriously consider it for the first time.'

'I don't get it.'

'What don't you get?'

'Your aversion to settling down.'

'I don't have an aversion to settling down. I have an aversion to the expectation most women have that settling down involves all that starry-eyed love nonsense.'

Shorn of the usual bantering, light-hearted tenor of their conversations, Gabriel heard the utter seriousness in his own voice with surprise. Despite the strong ties of friendship that bound them, there were certain lines that had never been crossed.

He was intensely private when it came to really talking about himself and what motivated him. He'd carried the scars of his childhood in silence for years and had never shared them with anyone.

Not even with Jennifer.

To do that would have meant exposing a vulnerable side to him he would always refuse to indulge. To be vulnerable was to open yourself up to the possibility of pain. He had seen how damaged his mother had been when she had handed herself over to a man who had abused her trust in him.

He had known the pain of hope being destroyed when he had gone on that unauthorised trip to see his father, only to find a stranger who wanted nothing to do with him.

Control over your life was everything because it protected you from being hurt.

The silence stretched between them, and Gabriel scowled.

'You're looking at me as though I've just told you I'm about to grow wings and fly to the moon,' he said.

'I'm shocked you could be so cynical, Gabriel.'

'Why?'

'Because…'

'My father walked out on us when I was a toddler,' he told her abruptly, a spontaneous response to the startled incredulity on her face at what he had said. 'He left my mother in mourning for a marriage that she had seen lasting a lifetime. He'd exploited her for her money, and I'm not sure she ever recovered from that betrayal. She certainly never looked for another relationship. It wasn't a great example of the power of love. In fact, it was a terrific example of what to avoid when it comes to trusting another human being to have your back.' He gave a cynical laugh.

'Your dad… I've never asked and you've never said. He never really kept in touch with you and your mother, did he? How is it that in all the years we've known each other, you've never talked about him?'

'There was never anything to talk about. The man disappeared without a backward glance.' Gabriel hesitated. She was right. He'd never opened up to her about that slice of his past, but now…

He shook his head, shedding the fuzzy temptation to keep talking.

'But,' Jennifer continued softly, 'divorce, sadly, is something that's very common. It doesn't mean that you have to lose your faith in love and marriage.'

'This is a pointless conversation. You need to drop it.'

His jaw clenched because he could see that his coldly harsh response had stung her. He raked his fingers through his hair and shifted uncomfortably. He'd forgotten about the glass of wine in front of him, but now he swallowed some and looked at her over the rim of the glass.

Her long, untamed brown hair was swept over one shoulder. She was strikingly attractive, had a face that spoke of intelligence, kindness and wit. A face and a personality that could suck you in if you weren't careful, but friendship or no friendship, he wasn't about to go soft round the edges and start searching for a shoulder to cry on.

More than that, there was a certain sexiness there. He felt a sudden, unaccustomed reaction to something he'd always, consciously or unconsciously, blocked out. Her physical appeal.

'You're curious about my lack of faith in love,' he drawled. 'I could ask you the same thing.' He smiled so that the atmosphere between them could get back on track. 'You're a catch, Jen, so why are you still single?'

Jennifer could read his intent, could follow the softening of his tone as he attempted to steer them away from suddenly turbulent waters. His sharp response had hurt, for some reason. A lot. It had also roused her curiosity. There had been something there, a darkness in his voice that had stirred her interest in ways she wouldn't have predicted.

Her curiosity felt dangerous. *He* felt dangerous. Unsettling.

'Prince Charming,' she responded teasingly, picking up his cue and going with it, 'is currently proving elusive. Maybe he can't find his trusty steed.'

But he had a point. Why was she still single? It was nice that he was polite enough to call her a catch, when his definition of *a catch* wasn't a very tall brunette who didn't think twice about arguing with him, but she was attractive. She knew that. So why did every guy she'd ever dated eventually prove disappointing?

'*However*,' she added stoutly, 'that doesn't mean that I'm like you. I *want* to settle down and have babies and make my mum a granny.'

'Which is perfect.'

'Sorry?'

'You and I are on completely different pages when it comes to our expectations in life. Yes, maybe there's a chance I'll settle down one of these days—and maybe sooner rather than later in view of everything that's happening right now—but…and this is a *big but*...if I do, it'll be with a woman who doesn't want what I'm not capable of giving.'

'You mean love and romance?'

'Precisely that.'

'Lucky girl. Does that person actually exist, Gabriel? If

you do a survey, I think you'll find that most women want the full package. Love, romance and stars in their eyes.'

'If you do a survey,' Gabriel responded wryly, '*I* think you'll find that the promise of limitless money would trump everything else.'

'You're so cynical.'

'Yes, I am, and this is why you're the only woman who could make this charade happen, Jen. We understand one another. You know who I am, and you understand my limitations. You could pretend to be my fiancée knowing that it's an illusion, something to build my mother's spirits and give her a reason for living. Once she's in a good place, she'll be mentally strong enough to deal with our eventual break-up and, like I've said, she'll be happily bolstered by the notion that I'm at last on the right track when it comes to settling down.'

'You make it sound so easy, Gabriel.'

'Because it is.'

He leaned towards her. Jennifer frowned at him, lost in her thoughts. She reached out, poked one finger against his chest and gently pushed him back.

'You're not giving me room to think.'

'Good.'

'How would this play out if I were to go along with your crazy scheme? Wait…what did you say about a vineyard?'

'You're on board,' Gabriel said with relief and satisfaction.

'I…'

'Good. You're doing the right thing.'

'Well…'

'Yes, I mentioned a vineyard. Tuscany. Beautiful this

time of year. The plan would be for us to go there, the three of us. I could check out the vineyard, my mother would get a much-needed opportunity to relax, and we could put on a good pretence of a couple in love away from nosy neighbours and prying friends.'

'You've really thought about this.'

'I'm a great believer in due diligence.'

'And where do we stay while you're checking out the vineyard?'

'The vineyard I'm interested in buying is on its last legs and attached to a rundown estate manned by an elderly couple. Their son isn't interested in taking it over, and they haven't got the funds to propel it into the next league. Good grapes, apparently, but not properly encouraged. We stay there. On site.'

'We stay there…on site…why do I feel as though the roller-coaster ride is picking up speed?'

'I admit I've sprung this on you, Jen, and I can't thank you enough for agreeing to do this with me and for me. It means a lot. We can return to how I financially show my appreciation in due course. For now, I can run through the basics so that we know how to play things.'

'There's no need to financially show me any appreciation,' Jennifer said distractedly.

She was in a daze, following the logic of his arguments while questioning why something so dubious could also make so much sense. Francesca was on cloud nine, and that was a good thing. Yes, in due course she would be disillusioned because the so-called engagement would eventually be called off, but by then…wasn't Gabriel right? She would be resilient enough to take it on the chin, especially if she knew that her son was finally appearing to be invested in dumping his playboy lifestyle? She would never know that any relationship he had going forward might not be a love match, but did that matter? Who was to say that a transactional relationship wouldn't outlast one that began with two people fancying themselves in love?

And as for their friendship? Nothing would change. If anything, wouldn't it deepen? He was right when he'd said that their dreams and hopes when it came to their own personal aspirations were very, very different.

They were conditioned to be two people whose relationship could never stray into anything other than friendship because they looked at life through different eyes.

When it came to phoney engagements, they were a match made in Heaven.

One day, when they were both happily married to other people, they would probably joke about it.

Nothing would be lost, and they would be doing a terrific thing for his mother who, yes, truly risked going rapidly downhill because everyone knew that stress could undermine recovery.

In fact, stress could literally be a killer.

Would Jennifer ever be able to live with herself if Francesca's health suffered because Jennifer refused to go along with Gabriel's well-intentioned plan, which had its roots in love and respect and a desire to do the best for his mother?

Also, Francesca had been so good to her own mother over the years. She would never know for certain, but Jennifer was sure that money had been lent years back that had enabled her mum to repel creditors banging on the door when mortgage repayments couldn't be made during the pandemic.

Wouldn't it be downright selfish of her to refuse to play ball?

'Tell me what you're thinking.'

Jennifer blinked and came back down to Planet Earth.

'You were telling me about this estate we would be staying in...' If there was a whisper of danger about the whole thing, then that must surely be in her imagination. There would always be an unbreachable chasm between them when it came to matters of the heart.

'Elderly couple, very old-fashioned...couldn't be better. We would have separate rooms because far be it from me to tread on the sensibilities of our kind-hearted, traditional Italian hosts who probably think that a couple sharing a bed before marriage is a punishable offence. I've met them a few times, and trust me, I know the score on that front. At any rate, I would be out for most of the day covering essential groundwork, seeing the actual state of the vineyards.' He grinned. 'I would do anything for my mother, but when it comes to the rest of the human race, I have my head firmly screwed on. If I can't see a way to making it pay, then the deal is off.'

'How long have you been thinking about this whole vineyard idea?'

'Actually, I started checking out the possibility of finding one over a year ago,' Gabriel confessed. 'And I seriously picked up pace on it about eight months ago when I located the one in Tuscany. Now it seems fortuitous, given the current situation. It'll be a very useful bolt-hole for my mother to get away from her daily grind and be exposed to something different. A change of scenery.'

They looked at one another in silence for a few seconds.

Jennifer felt a shiver ripple through her, a mixture of trepidation and simmering excitement as the unexpected opened up beneath her. 'When would this trip to Tuscany take place? I can't just jump to attention and drop everything without warning.'

'Why not? You're on school holidays. You have two months of doing nothing.'

'You know absolutely nothing about teaching,' Jennifer scoffed. Gabriel shot her one of those smiles that she always suspected the women he dated would have found devastating.

'I know you don't have to get up tomorrow morning at seven thirty to go to work,' he purred smoothly. Then he grinned. 'I can tell you're about to give me a lecture on all your responsibilities.' The grin widened. 'You can bring your books and prep your classes while we're in Tuscany, although my bet is you won't do any of that. You and my mother will doubtless want to see the countryside and explore all the villages while I'm busy during the day.'

Jennifer gasped. 'How long are you planning on us being there?'

'How long is a piece of string?'

'That's not an answer.'

Gabriel burst out laughing and shot her an appreciative look from under his lashes.

'I like the way you don't tiptoe around me,' he drawled,

laughter gradually subsiding. 'Thank God I don't have a fragile ego or I'd have been a broken man a long time ago.'

'Very funny, Gabriel.'

'When you think about it,' he mused, head tilted to one side, 'you might imagine my mother would be naturally sceptical about our newfound love given the history of the women I've dated in the past, but she's never had much time for those women. I admit I saw her trying not to snigger when the last one I brought to the house tried walking around the gardens in winter wearing ballet pumps. Very fetching in a sitting room but a little impractical in the great muddy outdoors. She's probably always nurtured the dream of a suitable woman being more like you.'

'Is there a compliment tucked away in there somewhere?' Jennifer asked tartly. Their eyes met, and the breath hitched in her throat.

God, the man was so sinfully gorgeous. Way too sexy for his own good.

Thank goodness, she reasoned belatedly, their friendship had made her immune to all of that.

'You know there is!' He beamed and then sprang to his feet. 'Right. I'm going to drop you back to your house. You have a lot to think about. We can fine-tune the details tomorrow.'

'You still haven't answered my question,' Jennifer said, scrambling to stand up and shoving her hair back. 'How long will we be gone? And don't tell me about pieces of string!'

'Ten days, max. I have too much on here to stay a day longer than that. By the end of our stay, I figure my mother will be hale, hearty and back to what she was before her heart problems.'

Except, Gabriel thought, had she really been hale and hearty before the heart problems? Or had he just seen what he'd wanted to see because digging any deeper would have opened a can of worms?

He spun round on his heels and glanced over his shoulder to Jennifer, who was pink and flustered and frowning as she hurried behind him.

For a few seconds, Gabriel was struck by what he had said earlier about his mother probably wanting to marry him off to a woman just like Jennifer.

She was attractive, *very attractive* in a striking, intelligent way. She had definite opinions and yet a tactful way of sharing her thoughts that was never at the expense of other people's points of view. A good listener. And for all that, she was still curiously feminine, with all that long, tangled hair and freckles and blue, blue, shrewdly teasing eyes.

He carried on looking and then frowned and abruptly looked away.

He could see why his mother would want to believe that he and his closest female friend might be an item. Suddenly it was very important for him to establish the boundaries between them.

He valued what he had with Jennifer and would never jeopardise it. Sure, the chances of doing that were nonexistent, because they both understood one another and understood why, on any kind of romantic level, they were utterly unsuited, but…

He *was* introducing a new element to their friendship.

Of course, it was fictional, but lines could get blurred. There was no way he wanted her to start thinking that she might ever be anything else other than his closest friend.

She surely wouldn't, would she?

For a second, just a second, he saw her as a woman filled with passion, turning those big blue eyes on him with hunger and sexual craving…

But no! Out-of-bounds. And, he thought cynically, for Jennifer, hunger and sexual craving didn't reside in a convenient box that could be open and shut at will. Hunger and sexual craving, for her, were tied up with love and marriage and permanence. She'd said so herself.

He stopped before opening the door which he had earlier closed and turned to her.

'I'm glad you're on board with this, Jen,' he said in a husky undertone. 'I could never trust any other woman to do this for me, to play this part. I would always fear that somewhere along the line, she would start…getting ideas, thinking that it might be a real relationship instead of a charade for the sake of my mother. But I know that with you…'

'You've already said this, Gabriel. There's no need to go over it. I know why you've come to me with this proposition. I'm a safe bet. We can play this game of make-believe, and then we can stop and things can return to normal, because we both know the rules of the game.'

'Well put.'

'I suppose we'll have to get our stories straight. Friends one minute, more than that the next? Does that ring true?'

'Of course it does. Friendship is a very sensible basis for a relationship.'

* * *

'So it is,' Jennifer murmured. She looked at him for a couple of seconds. It occurred to her just how one-sided his take on things had been.

He'd been very careful to remind her that this was all a charade, that it was a game in which only she could be a suitable participant because she would be the only woman to know the rules and to know how to obey them. No personal involvement. No thinking that what was a pretence might turn into something real.

As if he hadn't made that clear, he'd obviously felt compelled to repeat the mantra just in case she...*forgot*? Did he honestly think that there was no woman alive who could possibly resist him were she to be in his presence for long enough?

For once, Jennifer felt stirrings of real anger at him for his sweeping assumptions.

She folded her arms and stared at him coolly.

'Honestly, Gabriel, you are the most egotistic man I've ever met in my entire life.'

She was half amused, half impatient when his jaw dropped and he frowned in open puzzlement.

'Come again? Egotistic? Me? I'm prepared to do the most selfless thing anyone could ever imagine because I care about my mother. Since when is that being an egotist?'

'I'm not talking about that.'

'What then?'

'I'm talking about the fact that you think it's necessary to keep warning me that I need to be careful. Do you honestly think you're such a catch that after years of friendship, I'm going to be just too weak and gullible to resist the lure of Gabriel Garcia when he pretends to show an interest in me for five minutes?' She laughed dryly. 'Honestly! Have you forgotten that on a romantic level, *you're just not my type*?'

'Was that what I was doing?'

'Yes, it was! What makes you think that I'm the one who needs warning off?'

'What do you mean?'

'Maybe,' she said with pointed challenge, '*I* should be the one doing the warning. Maybe *you* need to be careful that you don't get it into your head that this charade you've set in motion is actually the real thing...'

'You're kidding.'

'Am I? You might think that you don't believe in love, that you're Mr Tough and Disillusioned, but everyone knows love creeps up on a person. You'd better be careful, Gabriel Garcia the Great, that it doesn't creep up on *you* just when you're not looking!'

'Never going to happen.'

'Good,' she returned silkily. 'Then there's no further need to warn me off, and I'll refrain from doing the same. Deal?'

'Deal.'

He reached out his hand and she did too. They shook on it, eyes locked.

'When this is over, things will return to being exactly the same between us,' he murmured. 'You have my word.'

CHAPTER FOUR

SUMMER RAINS, WHICH THE weathermen had been promising with unseemly gusto for the past week, arrived in force on the day they were leaving for Tuscany.

'Gardeners have been praying for a downpour!' they had boomed on the television, pointing to large swaths of the country due for a drenching that would last well beyond the weekend. 'They're in for a treat!'

Francesca, who had always been consumed by weather patterns because she was such an avid gardener, could barely muster an interest. All those plants that had been curling up in the dry heat? Oh dear.

'I have far too much on my mind at the moment,' she twittered with high-pitched, girlish excitement the night before when they had all sat down to dinner together. 'George will be fine looking after the garden for a while. They're only plants, after all.'

Now, waiting in the hall for Francesca and Gabriel, Jennifer contemplated the forthcoming ten days in a vineyard with strangers with consternation.

She had driven over with her bags having vaguely told her mother that she would be going to Italy with Gabriel and Francesca, not on holiday *as such*, but because she had the time now that she was on summer break from school and Gabriel had thought that his mother could do with the company and the change of scenery.

'He's going to be working out there,' she had said as she'd tried to dodge minefields and stick to the truth as much as she could, 'and I'll be with Francesca…er… keeping her company. You know she's been down in the dumps recently, and a change is as good as a rest!'

Her mother had looked understandably startled at plans that had come out of the blue, without warning, but she'd barely managed to get a word in as Jennifer had waxed lyrical about Francesca needing a break…and Gabriel, *isn't he a brilliant son*, thinking of her coming along because he *knew that she'd always wanted to go to Italy and how wonderful it would be for his mother to have her along...*

She and Gabriel had agreed that his mother was to keep the business of any upcoming announcements of an engagement to herself. He had told her, just before they'd parted company the night before, that he would take care to explain to his mother why their relationship had to be kept under wraps. Top secret…hush-hush… don't breathe a word…

She heard the sound of footsteps and glanced up at the impressive staircase to see them both heading down with Gabriel in front, carrying Francesca's bags.

A Louis Vuitton suitcase and a matching pull-along.

Their eyes met, and Gabriel could instantly spot Jennifer's nervousness. She was smiling, but the smile was a little too upbeat, too many teeth on show. Brittle. He knew her so well.

She was in a pair of light, ankle-length khaki trousers

and a navy blue short-sleeved T-shirt that was cropped and fitted loosely to the waist. Her hair was tied back into a plait at the back, and if she was wearing any make-up, then it was minimal. She looked much younger than her age. Was it the scattering of freckles? He didn't know. She'd always looked younger than her age. Even when she'd been seventeen, leggy and outdoorsy and always with that long mane of hair…

She'd had a day and a half to change her mind. He'd almost been surprised that she hadn't, because he knew that what he was asking of her was a lot. There were favours and then there were *favours*.

But at least he'd managed to persuade her to accept financial compensation from him.

Of course, she'd dug her heels in and refused, but in the end he'd convinced her that it would be for the best.

'It's not just about helping you out for the sake of helping you out, Jen,' he'd told her. 'You know I've told you countless times that I'm willing to give you or lend you the money to buy a place of your own, but this is different. This time I'm asking you to do something for me. If I pay you for what I'm asking you to do, then it stops being a favour and becomes a business transaction. Better that way. Keeps things nice and tidy.'

So here they were now. On their way to Italy. All systems go. Happy mother…more or less happy friend… and his stress levels, thankfully, were down to near zero.

His mother had flown down the final stairs, lively as a cricket now that she was no longer fretting about him and thinking about the grandchildren she was never going to have.

By the time he very slowly hit the bottom of the staircase, there had been hugging and chatter and a couple more hugs. Jennifer had managed to usher his mum through the door, handing her over to Gabriel's driver, who was there with an umbrella so that they wouldn't get wet as they walked towards the car. They would be flying on Gabriel's private plane.

'Well?' Jennifer whispered as she ducked out of the insistent drizzle, taking shelter in the doorway with its portico, 'Have you told her?'

'You mean that it's all top secret? Don't breathe a word? Walls have ears?'

'This isn't funny, Gabriel!'

'No, it's not. We're also not undercover secret agents exchanging time-sensitive information. We can look natural when we have a conversation. In fact, it would be very convincing if we look natural instead of conducting our conversations in dramatic whispers. Relax. It's all going to be fine.'

'That's easy for you to say,' Jennifer grumbled. They were both standing back, still by the front door, while Francesca was ushered towards the car and helped in.

'You take life too seriously. Always have. Look at my mother. She's complaining about me having too many cars. Haven't heard her complain like that in months. Anyway, rest assured, all is well. I've obeyed your instructions like a good little boy, and my mother is duly sworn to secrecy.'

'I know you're being sarcastic, but good. That's clever. Not making it out to be anything definite. Just something that's casual.'

'Not that casual.'

'Casual enough to have an ending in a few weeks' time,' Jennifer insisted.

'Are you having sudden misgivings?' Gabriel asked sharply.

'No. I told you I would go through with this and I wouldn't let you down now. Besides, it feels a little too late to come clean anyway.'

Gabriel half nodded. He looked past her to where his mother was now happily settled into the back seat of his black Range Rover, contentedly glancing across at them as they chatted by the door.

She looked the best she'd looked in…in as far back as he could remember.

'My mother looks like a different woman,' he murmured absently, re-focusing on Jennifer and then letting his eyes linger on her earnest, pink-cheeked face, and then noticing all sorts of sweetly endearing things that had got imprinted in his head over the years…the soft curve of her mouth, the tiny mole on her cheekbone, those adorable freckles…

'Doesn't she? I haven't seen her wearing makeup and dressing as though she really cared about how she looks in…'

'A hell of a long time?'

'A hell of a long time,' Jennifer parroted quietly.

Their eyes collided, bright blue and bottomless black.

'I'm really grateful,' Gabriel murmured sincerely, 'that you're doing this for me, Jen. I know I've said that before, but I can't say it enough. Just seeing my mother today has made me realise…' He raked his fingers through his hair and shook his head briefly, frowning.

'Realise what?'

'Realise how badly I took my eye off the ball,' he confessed heavily. 'Not just over the past few weeks and months, but over the past few years. She worried about my prioritising work over everything else, and she worried about the fact that I flitted from one woman to another, but she never made a big deal of it. It was easy not to pay attention to the little remarks she made.'

He wondered…but before he could be tempted into saying anything, he was interrupted by Jennifer saying sharply, 'Don't. You mustn't.'

His driver was scurrying over with the umbrella, which Gabriel took from him, but they didn't rush to the car. Despite the rain, the atmosphere was warm and sticky. He wasn't ready to drop the conversation yet.

'Don't what? Mustn't what?'

'Don't think that worrying about you had anything to do with your mother's health issues.'

The observation dropped into the space between them, leaving a brief but electric silence in its wake. All of a sudden, Gabriel realised that had been exactly what was going through his head.

Had been for a while.

Had maybe even accounted for his urgency in wanting Jennifer to agree to do what he'd asked her to do, pretend a relationship that might give his mother something to hold on to.

Had he somehow been responsible for his mother's heart problems?

It made him hark back to those dark times when, as a young child, he'd wondered whether he'd been responsible for his dad running off, before he'd realised that he'd had nothing to do with the terrible choices his father had made.

Jennifer had read his mind. For a few seconds, Gabriel was shaken by the accuracy of her observation. Did he like that? Well, he was rather uneasy with it…

'Okay. Let's make a run for it. Or walk. The rain seems to be giving up. So much for the accuracy of weather reports.'

'I know. They're always wrong. When they say storm, I plan for a picnic.'

Gabriel laughed, and then she felt the weight of his arm over her shoulders. Her whole body tensed because she hadn't been expecting any physical contact between them, and yet of course there would be some!

'Did you just stiffen up on me?' he whispered into her ear as they reached the car. 'We should try and do away with the tension. Doesn't fit in with a couple in love.'

'I'm not tense at all. As a matter of fact, I couldn't be more relaxed…' but the sensation of his arm over her shoulder lingered all the way to the airfield where Gabriel kept his private jet. She knew that it was usually housed closer to London, where he lived, but he'd flown it up a few weeks ago when he'd visited his mother and left it there.

She'd never been on his private plane. Like a lot in Gabriel's life, she now thought, it was just another show of wealth she knew about but had never actually experienced first hand.

Private jet…super yacht which she knew was moored somewhere or other and used now and again…vast mansion in Chelsea, naturally…houses in various countries…cars galore, garaged on every continent…

She knew about all his possessions and had often teased him about them over the years, telling him that he was such a spoiled child if he needed a million and one expensive toys, but she had never been anywhere near any of those expensive toys.

She'd been to his Chelsea house a couple of times when she'd gone with his mother and hers. He'd got them all tickets to see *The Nutcracker*, and they'd been spoiled rotten while they'd been there on their overnight stays. Then she'd returned to her little house in Sussex, and that vast Chelsea mansion had quickly been forgotten. She hadn't much liked it anyway. Too big, too polished, too white, too minimalist.

Now, as the car approached the airfield, as she saw the black-and-gold jet poised on the tarmac runway, she was forcibly struck by just who Gabriel Garcia was, beyond being the friend she'd known for years.

He was a tycoon, equally feared and respected. He was a billionaire who could change people's lives with a tap of his finger. This toy, which she had teased him about, was a symbol of his status, his power and his reach. She shivered when she thought about that, thought about that side of him she had never really glimpsed.

No wonder those little blonde, fluffy things clung to him like limpets, adoring and willing to do whatever he wanted. Money impressed. Private jets impressed.

She refused to be impressed. She'd never been impressed before, and she wasn't about to start now, although it was still disconcerting on some deep, barely there level to see up close the tangible evidence of just how wealthy and powerful he was.

Francesca had been absently chatting about the vagaries of the English weather, and Jennifer had been responding while her mind had leapfrogged over this, that and the other. Now, as the Range Rover slowed to a stop and as they hurried towards the waiting plane, she could tell that the older woman was beginning to flag.

A combination of overexcitement and a body still in recovery mode.

But wow, she looked tremendous compared to how she had looked a few weeks before. A few *months and years* before.

She was naturally a tall, elegant woman. Ill health had made her gaunt. Allowing her blond hair to go grey had aged her, but it was pulled back now, highlighting her high cheekbones. There was colour in her cheeks.

In an outfit of cream silk trousers and shirt, she looked fabulous.

'I can tell you're exhausted,' Jennifer said with consternation as soon as they were on the plane. 'Is this all too much?'

'Exhausted, but I couldn't be happier, my dear…'

Jennifer smiled and tried to think how she could take the happiness down a notch or two so that the older woman didn't get completely stuck in la-la land.

She didn't want to hurt the woman she dearly loved, but an injection of reality now and again wouldn't be a bad thing. Would it?

'Good, good,' she murmured as Francesca settled into the leather seat. 'Maybe you should…have a sleep. It's going to be a long day ahead, meeting new people and being out of the country.'

'Perhaps,' Francesca smiled, 'but you two will be there, and that's what will keep my spirits up.'

'Oh, you should never rely on other people to keep your spirits up!' Jennifer said brightly. 'In the end, you only have yourself to rely on. That's the philosophy I try to live by.'

Francesca's eyes were closing. Jennifer stood up and glanced around her for the first time since she'd stepped into the jet.

It was all fine leather, polished wood and brushed metal. The seats were large with footrests, and there was a clutch of sofas to the side. It was a compact space, big enough for maybe a dozen people, and bore no resemblance to the inside of any plane Jennifer had ever been on in her life.

Still absorbed in looking around her, she felt Gabriel's hand on her shoulder and then heard him murmur into her ear with amusement.

'Not meaning to rush your inspection of the surroundings, but the pilot's waiting to take off…'

Jennifer spun round, reddening. Gabriel was grinning. He gestured to two seats behind where his mother was beginning to nod off.

'Let's go sit there. Want anything to drink?'

Jennifer blinked and saw a blonde girl smiling at them.

'You have a flight attendant on board?'

'How else will I get my flute of champagne?'

'So true,' she said dryly, moving towards the seat and then settling into it before turning to face him. 'I think having to pour your own drink for yourself is beyond the pale. I can't believe you own this, Gabriel.'

'You know I own a private plane. You've enjoyed many a conversation telling me that I'm ruining the planet while I've tried to convince you that sometimes speed is of the essence.'

'Yes, but I never really took that on board. It was just something else you owned. It's amazing.'

'Does that mean you finally find me impressive?'

I've always found you impressive was the confusing thought that raced through Jennifer's mind, as fleeting as quicksilver, gone before it could take hold and demand further inspection.

'Absolutely not.'

'Shame. Well, you'll have to pretend over the next few days. I have a feeling being impressed with the person you're supposed to be in love with, at least when you're in the honeymoon stage, is obligatory. I heard the pep talk, by the way.'

'What pep talk?'

The engines had begun to rev, and the plane began its slow move towards take-off. Outside, dark, leaden skies had replaced the rain. Leaning into one another as they talked felt strangely cosy.

Which it was, in a way, Jennifer thought. It was the cosiness of two people plotting and deceiving.

'The one you gave my mother about not relying on other people to make her happy.'

'I was only being truthful. Besides, it's never too early to start laying the groundwork. Now that we're here, I'm beginning to feel seriously guilty about the whole thing. The sooner we end it, the better.'

'We have a deal.' Gabriel's voice was lazy but laced with steel. 'The eventual, inevitable break-up will require a prelude. Think of it as a play in three acts, with a beginning, a middle and an end.'

Jennifer's eyes widened. She again glimpsed that tycoon, the guy who ruled an empire and went through life getting exactly what he wanted.

The guy with the iron fist inside the velvet glove.

'Okay,' she conceded. 'I guess that's what you're paying me for.' It was the sort of thing she would never have said, least of all to Gabriel. She went bright red and mumbled a vague apology. His dark eyes, lasered on her, made her feel a little disoriented. 'That sounded a lot worse than I intended,' she finally admitted with a weak smile. 'I can't believe I was so mean and sarcastic.'

'You can't be sunshine and light all of the time.'

'Is that what you think of me? That I'm always sunshine and light? Little Miss Cheerful?'

'Don't look so offended.' He smiled and relaxed back into the deep leather seat, half closing his eyes. 'Last I heard, being cheerful wasn't a crime against humanity.'

Jennifer shot him a glassy smile, but he wasn't looking at her.

Crime against humanity? No, it wasn't, and he hadn't meant to be offensive. He really did see her as sunshine and light, and yet…wasn't that a one-dimensional picture of her? Did he think of her as a person who had no sides to her? No hidden places? No deep mysteries? No doubts or fears or unmet longings and desires? No regrets?

Why did she somehow think that in this instance, *cheerful* was on a par with *boring*?

'Do you want to tell me exactly what you said to your

mother about us? She must have quizzed you about how this whole ridiculous so-called love affair was supposed to have happened, and why it's now vital that we keep it under wraps.' Did he find her dull? They laughed a lot together, but was that, somehow, the sign of the eternally upbeat bore? 'I guess we need to get our stories straight so that we don't end up contradicting one another. And by the way, I'm not sunshine and light all of the time!'

Silence pooled between them.

'Where did *that* come from?'

Jennifer inwardly winced at whatever impulse had driven her to say what she'd just said. He'd straightened, opened his eyes and was staring at her with his head tilted to the side and a questioning look.

'Doesn't matter,' she muttered with a hint of defensiveness.

'Well, tut-tut, it does, in fact.'

'Why?'

'Because if we're supposed to be involved with one another on a romantic level, then surely I would need to know more about you than is currently on offer. So that our charade is all the more believable.'

It hadn't occurred to Gabriel that Jen might be offended by what he'd said. He enjoyed that she was straightforward. He liked the fact that she occupied the unique position in his life of being the only woman on the planet who never tried to impress him.

He liked that she was never moody, that she never took out her frustrations on him. Over the years, he'd rarely cancelled any dates he made with her, but when he had, she'd shrugged it off as no big deal.

So yes, she *was* sunshine and light but…wasn't she a lot more than that, too?

'You're smart,' he said a little uncomfortably, 'and funny, Jen. You know that. I'm pretty sure I've told you that in the past.'

'You look as though you're having to walk on a bed of nails to say that.' But she smiled and then chuckled. 'I don't mean to make you feel uncomfortable, Gabriel.'

'Why would that make me feel uncomfortable?'

'Because you're not a guy who does a lot of talking about feelings.'

'How do you know that?' Gabriel asked, amused and curious. 'You have no idea what conversations I have between the sheets with the women I make love to. I might be big into talking about feelings in bed.'

A slow burn started in Jennifer's body, rising in a hot tide through her veins until her head was throbbing and her mind was filled with all sorts of forbidden images.

Her throat went dry. For a few seconds, every coherent thought was submerged in a series of graphic images.

The reality was that he represented just the sort of guy who should never stir sexual interest. The uncomfortable truth was that right now, the fierce response of her body was saying otherwise.

'You're right.' She looked away, but she knew that she was as red as a beetroot. 'I don't know.' Just for good measure, she added, 'Nor am I all that interested.'

'Now whose turn is it to be uncomfortable?' he teased softly.

'This isn't what we're supposed to be doing,' she protested. Her heart was beating fast, and there was a weird sensation of struggling through quicksand as the parameters of their cosy relationship shifted, taking her into different territory. 'We're not supposed to be making one another feel uncomfortable. We're supposed to be going over the basics of what we say to your mother so that our stories are in sync. Maybe we should stick to that?'

'Of course.'

'While your mother's sleeping and before we land.'

'Good idea.'

But he was looking at her with lazy amusement. The more his dark eyes lingered, the more hot and bothered she felt.

'So just tell me what you said to her.'

'I didn't go into a lot of details,' Gabriel admitted, straightening. 'I just said that you and I, after all these years, had discovered a romantic connection.'

'*Discovered a romantic connection?* How? Where? Under a rock? Behind a tree? Surely you were a little more forthcoming than that?'

'I thought it best to keep the details to the minimum.'

'You're probably right, although I'm shocked she bought into that. And what was her reaction to our sudden awakening to love?'

'Remarkably little surprise and a whole lot of joy and rapture.'

'And what else? When did this miraculous realisation happen between us?'

'Again, I thought it best to keep that vague, especially considering that the last time I saw you, you were on a hot date.' He grinned. 'Any word from the rejected caveman?'

'I'm going to ignore that because you know the answer. I guess you and I could say we met up a couple of weeks ago, and one thing led to another.'

'Could work,' Gabriel mused thoughtfully. 'A deep and longstanding friendship…suddenly, over a bottle of wine, a dawning realisation…and then the rest, as they say, will be history. Until it's not. Where do you suggest the big reveal happened?'

'In London somewhere?'

'Shocking from the woman who rarely strays into the big bad city.'

'I don't think that's the right attitude for a besotted man to show his partner, do you?'

'Ah, I'm besotted. Fair enough.'

'And stop looking so amused,' Jennifer hissed. 'This is serious. I hate doing it, but if we're to go through with it, then we have to be committed about it!'

'You're right. Of course. Yes. We met in London. You came up for the day to go with me to a social function. I needed a plus-one, but more than that, we'd been meeting up off and on over the past few months. Suddenly I realised that I wanted to get to know you as more than just a friend.'

'Okay.'

'It's very fortunate that I haven't been in a relationship for the past few months,' he reflected.

'Very fortunate and also quite surprising,' Jennifer couldn't help teasing. 'Why the sudden bout of celibacy?'

Gabriel winced. 'Maybe I was already getting a little tired of my dating scene.'

'You mean there's such a thing as too many cute blondes hanging on to you for dear life?'

'Some men are only satisfied with cute blondes until they meet the right woman,' Gabriel murmured. 'Look at us! Who'd have thought?'

'Who indeed. And you mentioned to your mother, you said, about not telling anyone…'

Jennifer was so absorbed in their conversation that she was barely aware of the pilot warning them they would be landing shortly and they were to buckle up. He cracked a joke about the announcement not being necessary considering there were only three of them on board and one was sound asleep while the other two hadn't left their seats.

'I laid it on thick,' Gabriel assured her. 'I told her that as this was just a fledgling relationship, it was important that we didn't go public with anything just yet. The fewer people who know about this, the better, and that's a direct quote.'

'I'm really pleased about that. I can't imagine what my mother would do if she thought that the two of us were an item.'

'What do you mean?'

'She'd be shocked.'

'Why? Tell me her opinion of me isn't that low, especially compared to the sort of…'

'Don't say it, Gabriel! I *do not* date *losers*!' She glared at him, and he smiled placidly back in return. Jennifer added honestly, 'It's just that I think she's always seen you as the boy living in the Big House. I know our mothers go back a long way, and so do we, but you have to admit we come from very, very different backgrounds.'

'What does that have to do with anything?'

He sounded so genuinely shocked that Jennifer relaxed and smiled. The inner turmoil of only a few minutes ago dissipated. She re-adjusted to the comfortable space they normally occupied. It felt so much safer.

'This is the first time I've ever flown in this private plane before…' She looked around her then back to him. 'Course, I've known that you've owned one. I've known that you use it when you need to get somewhere fast—just like I know you have a superyacht and that you probably impress women with when you take them on it. But this is your world, and I'm a bystander looking on now and again.'

'I don't have to produce a superyacht from under my sleeve to impress women. Anyway, I'm still not following you. What does money have to do with anything? At any rate, it's not as though I haven't asked you to go on my plane in the past. It would have been a far more convenient way of transporting the three of you the last time you were in London to see that ballet production.'

'*The Nutcracker.* That was amazing.'

'So I'm a guy who's out-of-bounds? Because I have some money? There's a word for that, isn't there? Oh yes, I know. *Inverted snobbery.* I correct myself. Two words.'

Jennifer looked at him reprovingly. The plane was beginning to descend. When she glanced past Gabriel out of the window, she could still see sky and, rising up below, the solid shape of land-mass, still distant but growing closer.

'It's not about snobbery. It's just…the way it is. I'm an ordinary person, living an ordinary life, in search of an ordinary partner. My mum's always known that, so all I'm saying is that she would be astonished if suddenly, out of the blue, you and I were to announce that we're romantically involved with one another.'

'My mother barely batted an eyelid.'

'It's about expectations, I guess.' Jennifer shrugged. 'Maybe your mother has seen you in and out of so many unsuitable relationships that she's just relieved to think you've found someone she likes for you as a partner. She knows me. She likes me. The expectations aren't the same.'

'And have you never wanted to blow the lid off expectations, Jen? To aim for more than just what you've always assumed was waiting in the future for you?'

'No,' she said flatly. 'Besides, who says that aiming for more than what I've always assumed is waiting out there for me means aiming for a guy with lots of money?'

'Touché.'

For just a second, a fleeting second, there was the fizz of electricity in their locked gazes, in the silence that was suddenly heavy with tension. Gabriel was the first to break the connection.

'We're landing,' he said, looking away. 'Don't worry, Jen. It'll be over in the blink of an eye, and things can return to what we both know.' His dark eyes softened as he rested them once again on her. 'This is just a part we're both playing. Before you know it, acts one and two will be done and dusted. The final act will be here, and it'll be the easiest to play…'

CHAPTER FIVE

GABRIEL HAD THOUGHT it all out, down to the finest detail. He'd been shocked and panicked by his mother's sudden show of vulnerability when, on the health front, good progress was being made after her heart scare.

She was stoic by nature. To have seen her break down had hit him very hard. She despaired of him? Despaired that she would die without seeing him settled? Couldn't see the point of anything?

It had felt as though the bottom had suddenly dropped out of his comfortable, well-ordered world, and he had been besieged with guilt. He'd looked back over his shoulder to his workaholic lifestyle, interspersed with casual relationships that came and went without leaving so much as a ripple. He'd thought about how work had prevented him from coming to visit as often as he'd wanted during her recent convalescence. No amount of video calling could make up for his absence.

He'd always thought he'd been doing the right thing. Working hard to restore and maintain the family finances, assuming the role of the responsible male in the family, bearing in mind the antics of his loser father. Therefore, to learn that his dedication to the massive responsibilities he'd carried on his shoulders had, in fact, been a growing source of unending stress to his mother had come as a severe shock to his system.

He had immediately gone into damage limitation mode and had prided himself on coming up with the perfect solution to the problem.

Foolproof, in fact.

A series of steps, all of which would lead to the desired outcome.

His mother wanted to see him in a serious relationship? Needed that for her to climb back on the road to full recovery? No problem. He would produce one for her benefit. No one from the proverbial little black book, because that would be inviting a whole world of potential trouble, but the one woman he knew he could always count on and, more importantly, the one woman he knew would fit the bill.

Jennifer.

Jennifer would agree because it would be no more than a harmless piece of fiction, and she loved his mother almost as much as he did.

Granted, that hadn't gone as smoothly as anticipated, but he'd got what he'd wanted in the end, and the fact that he'd persuaded her to accept money for what she'd be doing was icing on the cake. Because it would draw a defining line between fact and fiction and turn it into a proper arrangement. He liked that. Aside from anything else, he'd wanted to help her out financially for a while and had never understood why she couldn't just accept the help he'd always been keen to give her. She really needed to find a place of her own.

Step two would be the vineyard. He would take them both there. Away from prying eyes, he and Jennifer could play the loved-up couple while his mother benefited from the change of scenery. Buying the vineyard had been in his sights for a while. He had developed a relationship with the owners, Luisa and Roberto. They were a traditional Italian family who had been making noises about meeting his family. It meant a lot to them that they sell to someone of whom they personally approved, because money wasn't everything.

What better solution than for them to all go there together, and Luisa and Roberto had leapt at the suggestion with alacrity.

It helped that they were traditional enough to ensure sleeping arrangements that suited a phoney relationship.

Separate bedrooms.

He was sure he'd heard them expressing horror at the thought of either of their daughters *living in sin*. Excellent principles when it came to ensuring that he and Jennifer were positioned on opposite sides of their house to avoid any hanky-panky. Or so he'd assumed.

So what could possibly go wrong?

'This isn't quite what I expected on the sleeping arrangement front.' He did a full circle of the private cottage they'd been placed in. It was far enough away from the main house to be completely private and was rustic and charming, with worn, pretty rugs on the floor and photos of the vineyard in frames on the walls. Inspection over, he finally stopped, his dark eyes landing on Jennifer, who was staring at him accusingly with her hands on her hips.

'I'm sure it isn't,' she said with dripping sarcasm and raised eyebrows.

'Life can be unpredictable,' he offered.

'Really? I thought you didn't like the unpredictable, so you always made sure to ambush it before it could show up unexpectedly on your doorstep and ruin your life.'

'How well you know me. I like that. Let's sit outside, admire the scenery and have a chat.'

Jennifer clicked her tongue with exasperation. Of course, true to form, he had barely raised an eyebrow when *the very traditional Luisa and Roberto* had proudly informed them that one of the cottages in the grounds had been set aside for them. This from the couple who, he had assured her, would never countenance a couple cohabiting unless rings were on fingers, church bells had been rung and vows had been made.

Francesca, they had said warmly, hugging her to their hospitable bosoms, would stay in the main house with them so that they could get to know her better.

Unless anyone objected.

No one had, including Francesca, who had been delighted because she'd taken to the older couple on sight. She, likewise, had bought into the idea that the lovebirds would appreciate time to themselves.

'I thought you knew Luisa and Roberto well enough to be certain that we would have separate bedrooms? Weren't they supposed to have strict ideas about couples not sharing bedrooms until they'd walked up the aisle?'

'We have separate bedrooms. In fact, I count three plus the office in this cottage. I suppose this was used for the manager of the vineyard before his role became redundant. Poor guy. Still, businesses fail. There's only a skeleton crew here, although I'm willing to give jobs to any of the old staff, as agreed with Roberto. What would you like to drink? Tea? Coffee? Brandy to blunt the shock?'

'You should have seen this coming.'

'Even I am infallible and can't predict the future.'

'I'll have coffee if there's any.' Jennifer gave up because she was getting nowhere, and there was no point allocating blame when the situation couldn't be changed.

And he was right. There were three bedrooms in the cottage. Yet…something about sharing a private space with him like this made the hairs on the back of her neck stand on end.

She'd already started noticing him in ways that made her heart beat just a little bit quicker, but she knew it was imperative not to dwell on any of that. It meant nothing.

She looked at him as he began checking cupboards and drawers in the compact kitchenette and then opening the fridge and inspecting the contents.

He turned to her and lounged against the fridge, having shut the door. 'I'm glad to see that they've provided us with an ample amount of red wine. I think this will have been laid down before the vineyard began running to seed. Should be good. I had some when I came here a few months ago to do a preliminary inventory of what I was letting myself in for. Sure you won't have a glass?'

'I've had enough for tonight,' she said. 'You were right when you said that they're a lovely couple, Gabriel. They are. And I suppose…' she cast an eye over the cottage, which was small and perfectly formed '…it was thoughtful of them to consider that we might want some privacy.'

'Agreed.'

'I didn't think your mother would be happy about that,' Jennifer admitted. 'I mean about staying with people she doesn't know at all when it wasn't in the original plan.'

God, he looks amazing, she absently thought as her eyes drifted idly over him. Designer-clad and coolly, effortlessly elegant. He looked as though he belonged here, here in this sun-drenched, beautiful country, but of course he would. His father had been Italian. She'd been too young when he'd left to remember what he had looked like, but she was assuming from the little she'd gleaned over the years that he'd been tall, dark and handsome.

Her mind did a little more wandering. She was brought back down to earth when she realised he was standing in front of her with a mug of coffee in his hand for her.

'She's going with the flow,' he reasoned.

'Yes, but...'

'Let's go sit outside. Balmy night. Nice view. We can talk a little more about the details of this arrangement. You can continue raising doubts, and I can continue knocking them back.'

He hadn't drunk much over the lovely dinner Luisa had prepared, but he had a glass of red wine in his hand now as he preceded her outside, where a cluster of wooden chairs were stationed to make the most of the expansive view of the vineyards. The sky was velvet black now and studded with stars, and the rustle of the breeze through the vines was a soothing background noise.

'I'm not raising doubts,' was the first thing Jennifer

said as soon as they were sitting side by side like the real couple they weren't. 'I was just expressing surprise that your mum was so keen to stay in the main house when we were out here.'

'It'll do her good,' Gabriel said thoughtfully. 'I've noticed just how much she's withdrawn from her social circle over the past few months. Luisa and Roberto are very welcoming hosts. She senses that and…what can I say? Some of her that was lost in depression is beginning to resurface. My mother, as you know, used to be a very sociable woman.' He turned and looked at her averted profile. 'Tell me you don't begrudge that.'

'Of course I don't.'

'Good. So now we've dealt with that misgiving, let's move on to the next.'

'Stop being annoying when I'm trying to be serious, Gabriel.'

Their conversation was lazy and good-humoured, but underneath that, she was still weirdly conscious of her body behaving differently, responding differently, as if every part of it was being lightly caressed by something soft and invisible.

His elbow, resting on the arm of his chair, was almost touching hers.

She was used to his proximity.

She'd known him for most of her life! And yet suddenly this was a man she didn't know, a man she felt she was discovering for the first time, who roused things in her she knew shouldn't be roused.

The only way to combat those peculiar feelings was to keep it light.

'The cottage,' he continued thoughtfully. 'Us sharing it. Slight hiccup because it's something I hadn't predicted, but I think it's going to work to our advantage.'

'Really?'

'Really. Think about it.' He sipped his wine and looked straight ahead, his body mirroring hers. 'The minute we're in here, there will be no need to pretend that we're a couple. We can revert to being the comfortable friends we've always been without my mother's eagle eye on us.'

'Trrrruuuueeeee...' She dragged the word out dubiously.

'I can sense a *but* there somewhere...'

'But it feels as though the more people are involved in this charade, somehow the more complicated it gets.' She turned to him just as he turned to look at her. In the moonlit semi-darkness with just the light from the cottage casting a glow from behind them, their eyes met and held.

Her mouth went dry. For a second, her thoughts became a little jumbled.

'And the more complicated it gets,' she continued in a hitched voice, 'the harder it's going to be to extricate ourselves from...from our so-called relationship.'

'You're over-thinking it, Jen. First of all, there aren't queues of people lining up to get involved and find out what's going on between us. Friends and family don't know a thing, and it'll stay that way. You're also projecting. What makes you think it's going to be difficult to extricate ourselves from this?'

'What makes you think it isn't?'

'Tut-tut, that's a very defeatist approach.'

'For someone so clever, Gabriel, sometimes you can be so...so...*obtuse*.'

'Sometimes seeing too much grey in the mix confuses things,' he returned comfortably. 'Right now, I'm taking it one day at a time. On this particular day, I see my mother with a smile on her face and an upbeat attitude that wasn't there a week ago.' He gently placed his glass on the ground next to his chair and relaxed back, arms folded behind his head. 'Stunning view, wouldn't you agree? Especially at night. Atmospheric.'

'Will you buy it?' she asked curiously.

'It'll happen.'

'Why?'

'Because I happen to be fond of red wine. So why not own a vineyard? It's not as though I can't afford it. As an added bonus, with the right management and the right amount of money thrown at it, it has all the hallmarks of making a substantial profit.'

'Don't you sometimes want to take a step back and start relaxing a bit more?'

She manoeuvred her chair slightly so that she could look at him without twisting around. The silence that greeted her question was pensive and serious.

He eventually countered her question with a question. 'Why would I do that?'

'Well, for a start, you could spend some more time with your mum and also…you know, when this phoney situation ends and you actually do decide to settle down, you're going to have to become accustomed to a life of less work and more…wearing an apron and doing the dishes.'

She shuffled back into her original position so that they were both now staring up at a starlit, moonlit sky and the never-ending dark, swaying shapes of the vines and the trees stretching out towards distant horizons.

The silence between them was comfortable, relaxed, and yet she was still conscious of the closeness of their bodies, the soft sound of his breathing, the length of muscular legs stretched out in front of him.

'Well, not necessarily,' he finally murmured. 'Like I told you, marriage for me would never look like marriage for you. I'm not on the lookout for my soulmate, and yes, life would change somewhat if and when I settle down…' He paused briefly. 'When. When I settle down. I'm not getting any younger, and my mother has opened my eyes to a future I thought was waiting round a few more corners up ahead. So *when* I settle down, it won't be with someone who expects me to give up work so that I can start doing DIY and pottering in the garden.'

Jennifer laughed drowsily. 'There's such a thing as the middle road.'

'Tell me about that.'

'I know you're not really interested, so why should I?'

'Because you can't resist when I ask you a question.' He chuckled. 'Too much temptation to disagree with me and engineer an argument.'

'Either I'm sunshine and light or else I'm someone who engineers arguments. I can't be both.'

'You're both with me. What are you like with those men you've dated in the past? Which persona do you adopt?'

Jennifer felt him shift position, and then she felt the laser burn of his dark eyes on her averted profile, but she wasn't going to let that lazy inspection get to her. She wasn't going to let her body disobey her head. She was going to be the friend he was accustomed to. She was going to ignore the shift she felt had mysteriously happened between them, which was probably only in her imagination anyway.

'I don't *adopt personas*,' she said dryly. 'I'm not a psychopath, Gabriel. Anyway, what personas do *you* adopt when you're with those girls of yours?'

'I think it's fair to say that neither of us are psychopaths, so I don't adopt personas either. Have you noticed that your voice always changes when you talk about the women I date? Why is that? I can always sense just a little bit of contempt in your tone.'

In the darkness, Jennifer flushed. Was he right? Surely not.

'Really?' she said airily. 'I can't say I've noticed.' She paused. 'If anything, maybe sometimes I can't help but be mystified as to why a guy as clever as you chooses to go out with women who don't seem to challenge you.'

'Depends on your definition of *challenge*,' Gabriel drawled. 'Anyway, I'm the same with everyone. Honest, straightforward and charming.'

'If you say so. Will you be going to do whatever you have to do with Roberto tomorrow? Have a look at vineyards? Get filled in on what might need doing?'

'I already have a pretty good idea of what's been happening here for the past few years and why it's ended up where it has,' he said. 'I've done a lot of due diligence already. Knowledge, as they say, is power. But yes, I think the days can play out like that. You'll be left with my mother and Luisa, if she wants to join, during the day. I'll arrange a driver. You can do a little exploring.'

'Right. So our make-believe game will only begin once you're back from your day's adventures.'

'That's the plan.'

'And first thing in the morning?' It occurred to her that she had actually never woken up in the same place as Gabriel, however many lunches and dinners with friends and family they had shared over the years, how many conversations and debates and arguments they'd had. 'I mean…just so we know the routine, what time do you wake up? Go to bed?' She laughed a little awkwardly. 'We've known each other for such a long time, yet it's surprising I don't know those details about you.'

'Why would you?'

'I…ah…'

'You'd only know those details if you were my lover and knew my intimate habits.' He fell silent for a couple of seconds. Then he added on a lighter note, 'But come to think of it, you're not alone in that. Very few people know my waking and sleeping habits. At a push, my executive assistant, but only because I'm always awake when she communicates with me, whatever the time of day or night. So she knows I go to bed late and wake at the crack of dawn.'

'And all your…er…lovers?'

'I don't usually do sleepovers,' he said kindly. 'I prefer an uncluttered bed.'

'Even when you go on holiday with someone? How does that work for you?'

'I can't tell you the last time I had a holiday with a woman.'

'But you've stayed over at your mum's with women in the past.'

'Interesting you know my comings and goings.'

'I don't! I… Francesca always tells me when you've been. It just crops up in conversation…now and again.'

She felt suddenly hot and bothered as his casual observation struck home. Oddly, she did seem to know a lot about what he was up to when she wasn't around.

'I always respect my mother's unspoken rules and establish whoever I'm with in a separate suite.'

'Very pious of you. I had no idea you were so old-fashioned.'

Gabriel grinned. 'At any rate, beyond that, separate sleeping quarters work because my hours can be unnerving if anyone has to put up with them. I hit the sack very, very late when I'm finished working, and I get up very, very early to continue where I left off. Often I have early morning transatlantic calls on speaker phone when I'm in the bedroom and moving around. Disconcerting if you're a partner trying to carry on sleeping at five in the morning. And when I *do* share a bed overnight with a woman? Up early and on the move before she's opened her eyes.'

Jennifer laughed and began standing up. She shot him a knowing look from under her lashes and held his gaze for a few seconds. 'You mean you don't want them getting any ideas. Too many cosy cups of morning coffee in bed and they might start looking for more than you want to offer.'

'Like I said, how well you know me.'

He remained where he was, watching her as she began moving away.

When the door clicked shut behind her, he left it a

while…sat thinking, sipping his red wine until he was certain she'd showered and was asleep.

She was alarmed by this new, unexpected arrangement, and why wouldn't she be?

They really knew nothing of one another's personal habits. Was she a morning person? A night owl? From that thought came another and another…

As he'd told her, he tried not to spend the night with any woman…or at least, the occasions were rare. He liked his personal space and could easily compartmentalise his solitary downtime, his work time and his play time.

Did *she* share her space with whatever man she happened to be dating?

She was gregarious and warm-hearted by nature. He was fundamentally intensely private.

But now they would be finding out a little bit more about one another. It wasn't a treacherous slope, but as he headed inside, quietly shutting the door behind him, and walked to his bedroom, he couldn't stop the feathery touch of trepidation.

Gabriel heard the faintest of noises and stirred instantly. He hadn't been asleep, but his mind had been drifting. He'd been thinking about Jennifer, not in a consciously analytical way but in a distracted, vaguely cloudy way with strands of thoughts coming together and pulling away.

Something in the atmosphere between them had changed. A subtle change that thrummed between them now like an invisible spark of electricity that made him feel over-alert and wired.

Sharing this cottage…

Unexpected. He'd seen the look of horror on Jennifer's face when Luisa had triumphantly told them that Francesca could stay in the main house so they had the cottage to themselves.

All of a sudden, it had felt as though his foolproof arrangement had been turned on its head.

How had that happened? He'd been so sure that everything would be straightforward.

Yet here they were.

He was uneasily aware of the adage about *best laid plans* but dismissed the thought as fast as it entered his head. His plans never went awry, and this had been a carefully thought-out plan.

He decided that the cottage sharing was a minor setback. Like he'd told Jennifer, at least there would be a reprieve from the playacting when they were on their own here.

He heard that stealthy noise again.

Distracted by his own unedifying thoughts and frustrated that he couldn't seem to get a handle on them, Gabriel padded to the door without switching his light on, only stopping to sling a towel around his waist in the absence of a dressing gown.

He pulled open his bedroom door softly.

He had no idea what he'd been expecting to find at three in the morning. An intruder? Creeping around in a remote cottage in the middle of nowhere?

His brain hadn't fully engaged when he looked out of the bedroom, but he saw her immediately, her back to him as she peered inside the fridge in search of…ah, a bottle of water. She'd been bending over, but now, with the bottle in her hand, she straightened, removed the cap and drank, head back and eyes closed.

Gabriel dragged in a shaky breath and stared, mesmerised. Her long, dark hair tumbled down her back to her waist, and her body…

He'd seen her in a million different outfits but never in a pair of pyjama shorts and a vest. The shorts were festooned with cartoon characters, and the vest was white and close-fitting. As she turned sideways, it showed off…

He breathed out and continued to stare.

He could feel himself hardening until his erection was so stiff that it hurt.

She wasn't wearing a bra, and the soft fullness of her breasts begged to be touched.

He was about to beat a hasty retreat back into his bedroom when she turned round fully, still drinking the water. Although the moment their eyes met, she stopped and slowly lowered her hand. A slow creep of colour seeped into her cheeks. Even in the half-light in the kitchenette, he could see that, was aware that she was blushing.

'I… I heard a noise,' Gabriel said with hoarse challenge in his voice. He didn't want to look at her breasts. He did his utmost not to, but he couldn't help himself, couldn't miss the way they hung, heavy and full. He could almost see the outlines of nipples.

Jennifer, staring back at him, wanted the ground to open and swallow her whole.

Every inch of her felt exposed, from her legs, on show in a way that felt more revealing than if she'd been wearing a swimsuit, to her breasts, which were bursting out of the miniscule vest. Even the fact that she was barefoot made her feel as if she was advertising all her womanly assets in a brazen invitation.

Gabriel had never seen her before like this, in surroundings like these, in a situation like this one…

It was intensely, shockingly intimate. As his friend, she shouldn't be standing here, mortified and acutely conscious of herself and of him in ways that made her toes curl. This was the guy who had seen her cry during a tearjerker, made her laugh when she'd been feeling down and listened to all her worries when she'd been starting out in her teaching job.

This was *her friend.*

'A noise?' was the sum total of what she could muster in response as she drank him up with greedy eyes. He was wearing nothing but a towel around his waist. Her eyes skirted over that completely. Too dangerous. Although was it any less dangerous staring at his hard, muscled chest? The broad, sinewy shoulders?

The dampness between her thighs intensified, and she was overwhelmed with a crazy restlessness.

'I just wanted some water.' She stumbled over her words, which immediately made her cross with herself and cross with him for making her cross. 'It's not a crime!'

'Obviously not.'

'Well, you're staring at me as though I've done something wrong. I know we've been forced into sharing this cottage, but you'd better tell me if there are certain rules that I need to obey, such as not tiptoeing out to get some water from the fridge!'

'Don't be ridiculous.' Gabriel raked his fingers through his hair and scowled. 'You can do whatever you want. Do you really think I care whether you get yourself some water or not? I heard a noise, and I came out to see what was going on in case it was an intruder.'

'Why would an intruder intrude here? And sorry if I snapped,' she mumbled. 'You startled me, that's all.'

'Apology accepted. I'm going to get back to bed.'

'Okay, and I'm going to…to…*finish drinking my water*. Good night! Or morning. Whatever.'

She turned her back to him, which didn't make her feel any less exposed. Now her bum was on show, and the shorts she was wearing were very brief indeed.

Gabriel remained rooted to the spot because the sight on offer now was too tempting.

Her full, rounded bottom, barely covered by the skimpy shorts, was frankly spectacular.

He imagined cupping those succulent cheeks in his hands and had to stifle a groan.

Instead, he spun round, fiercely angry with himself for his lack of self-control, and made sure she heard the door shut firmly behind him.

Jennifer heard the click of his bedroom door and finally managed to breathe properly. She slowly turned around. Yes, thankfully, the small living area was empty.

What had just happened here?

She knew. He'd stood there in all his glorious, hunky, masculine beauty, and she'd *fancied him*.

She tiptoed back to her bedroom, head buzzing with thoughts that refused to be reasoned away.

She'd crossed a line. He'd innocently come out to check the place because he'd heard something, and he'd caught her in the kitchen. And instead of laughing and teasing him, which was how any friend would have responded, she'd gone into some kind of ridiculous panic attack.

Her eyes had swept over him, taking in the bare chest, the long legs, the low-slung towel around his narrow waist. Although she'd looked away immediately and done her utmost to keep her disobedient eyes on his face after that, the memory of what she'd seen had been imprinted in her mind with the force of a branding iron.

Disgusted with herself, she lay down on the bed and stared angrily at the ceiling.

The whole crazy situation was getting to her in ways she hadn't anticipated, but she was here now, and she was going to have to deal with it. Fancying Gabriel? A joke. She'd obviously just responded to the sight of a half-naked sexy guy three metres away from her.

Her last date had been the biker! And before that, an accountant who had nearly made her fall asleep. And before that? A lecturer she'd met at a teacher's convention in Leeds who had asked her out and then practised his profession on her by lecturing to her about his passion, which happened to be cycling.

So Gabriel? The guy who was too hot for his own good?

No surprise that she had had a passing moment of feeling out of her depth.

But she couldn't let a passing moment muddy the water. Gabriel, as a friend, was great. Gabriel in any other capacity was not only taboo but also just the sort of man she could never be interested in.

She wanted, more than anything else, a committed, serious relationship. She knew that the men she chose had not lived up to expectation in the past, but that didn't mean that she went out with them without hope in her heart. Hope that this would be the one. Hope that all the love she knew she had to give would find a worthy recipient. If she was disappointed time and again, then that was the nature of dating, and she never lost faith that the day would come when she would find The One. Her parents had had that. She had seen what love was all about. That was what she wanted for herself.

Gabriel had no time for any of that. For him, no such thing existed.

They couldn't have been at more opposite ends of the spectrum.

So tomorrow? She would have to listen to common sense and put that momentary distraction behind her. She would have to be the friend he had always known.

She finally fell asleep. When she woke, it was to find that the cottage was empty and it was late. After ten.

She dressed quickly. Mindful of what he had last seen her in, she hesitated and then shoved on a shapeless summer dress that fell to her calves and did a decent job at concealing all her curves.

She hurried over to the main house to find Luisa and Francesca in the kitchen, where they were finishing breakfast and the staff that Gabriel had hired were cleaning and tidying and making themselves useful. There were also nice smells in the kitchen, so she thought that perhaps some early-hours cooking and baking had been done.

Gabriel was nowhere to be seen because he'd vanished wherever with Roberto.

A new day was beginning, and it was time to get her thoughts in order and see this thing through without any more panic attacks…

CHAPTER SIX

JENNIFER FOUGHT OFF a landslide of near-impossible-to-answer questions during the course of the day.

By five in the evening, she was beginning to think that inspecting a vineyard and going through business accounts was definitely the very, very long straw, and what she had drawn was the very, very short one.

On cue, after an amazing breakfast, she and Francesca had headed out to see some of the countryside and visit one of the towns known for its perfectly preserved medieval architecture and breathtaking views. Luisa knew it well and had rattled off a list of places they could visit and cafés and restaurants where they could stop to drink some of the best coffee in Tuscany and eat some of the best pasta on the planet.

'You enjoy yourself,' she had instructed Francesca in a no-nonsense voice. Jennifer had smiled warmly because she just couldn't help it. 'And try the Crostata at the bakery in the piazza.' She'd kissed her fingers to express just how delicious they would find the tart. 'Tell Nonna Agostini that Luisa sent you. She will give you an extra one for free!'

If Jennifer had had her way, the entire day would have

been spent talking about architecture, gazing at views and eating pastries.

A lot less of a minefield than the barrage of questions she'd found herself trying to field.

The questions, in true Francesca fashion, had been softly spoken and sweetly curious, which had almost been worse than if she had opted for a bare lightbulb, a hard chair and a lie detector machine to eke out whether there were any gaps in the story being told.

By the end of the day, as they'd headed back to the vineyard in the chauffeur-driven car supplied by Gabriel, she felt as though she'd been through the wringer several hundred times.

Now, with Francesca and Luisa in the kitchen catching up over some fresh lemonade and home-baked cake, Jennifer was finally free to head back to the cottage.

It had been a gloriously warm day with just enough of a breeze to make sightseeing comfortable. For all that, though, she still felt weary and mentally drained and then, as she approached the cottage, nervous about seeing Gabriel again.

Memories of their encounter had nudged at the back of her mind throughout the day. Staving off some of Francesca's more misty-eyed predictions for a future that definitely wasn't in the cards had taken up a lot of mental energy, but still… Underneath the tension of stepping through minefields to try and avoid outright lying, the simmering recollection of Gabriel standing there in the room, looking at her with that veiled, unreadable expression… With his sheer physical beauty, the leanness of his hips and the breadth of his shoulders…

She couldn't clear her head of the rousing images.

Then she thought of herself, wearing next to nothing, feeling exposed and on show, and she cringed.

She pushed open the cottage door. As soon as she entered, she spotted Gabriel in the office. The desk faced out to the small entrance area. He looked up when she walked in, and their eyes tangled for a few silent seconds. Suddenly she was no longer tired, sticky and mentally drained. Rather, she was energised, all senses on full alert.

Looking at her, Gabriel could feel the steady uptick of his heartbeat and the stirring of an arousal that went completely contrary to everything in his head, to every scathing inner talk he had given himself during the course of the day.

This woman was not up for grabs, and it was shameful to even see her in that light—yet he was finding it impossible to forget the impression she had made on him the night before.

Her body had fired him up in a way he hadn't experienced in a long, long time. Just like that, he had been catapulted back to adolescence and to the horniness of a teenage boy with way too many raging hormones and not enough maturity to control them.

She wasn't dressed in next to nothing as she hovered in the entranceway now, but he was still fired up. She was in a dress that couldn't have looked sexier, although it was doing its best to hide her luscious curves.

'I'm working,' he said brusquely.

'I…'

Gabriel immediately felt like a complete bastard. Was it her fault that his body was playing games with him?

No. Whether money would change hands or not, she was there as a favour to him. He stood up, pushing back the chair, and swung round it to walk towards her.

'Sorry, Jen.'

She smelled of sunshine. Her cheeks were pink. Her hair, which had started the day neatly tied back, he presumed, was now tousled around her face. He had an insane urge to push the wayward strands back, tuck them behind her ears and then pull her towards him.

Her blue eyes looked bluer than usual, her lashes darker, her mouth fuller and pinker.

'Got back a little over an hour ago,' he expanded in a roughened undertone, 'and I'm catching up on a couple of thorny issues on the work front.'

'Okay.'

'Tell me about your day, or would you rather head for the shower? You look as though you could do with one. It's hot out there.'

Looking at him, Jennifer could sense his discomfort. He was normally so cool and collected. Utterly immune to nerves. Now, though, there was an edginess to him as he raked his fingers through his hair, his dark eyes skirting away from looking at her directly.

There could only be one reason for the way he was acting. He was embarrassed. Embarrassed that he had caught her rummaging in the fridge wearing almost nothing. Mortified on her behalf. He'd seen her practically in the raw, and she wondered whether he had been just a little bit repulsed at the sight. She didn't think so, had never been self-conscious in his presence, and it annoyed her that she was now.

Jennifer shuddered to think how he would react if he had the slightest inclination of some of the lascivious thoughts that had flashed through her head ever since she had seen him in nothing but a towel.

She decided that reverting to the easy familiarity they'd always shared would be the best solution to try and recover normality.

'What are you trying to tell me?' she teased, finally ungluing her limbs and heading to the kitchen so that she could fetch something cold to drink. 'That I look really sweaty?' She laughed gaily with her back to him as she drank some water, then quickly rinsed the glass and stuck it on the draining board by the sink. When she turned to look at him, she leaned with her back to the sink, hands tucked behind her.

She kept the cheerful smile pinned to her face.

'We ladies have very fragile egos, you know,' she chided. 'But seriously, it was hot out there, although your mum and I did enough sitting in between sightseeing so that she didn't get too exhausted.'

'How was it?'

He spun round and strolled towards the sitting room, moving to sit on the deep, comfy sofa and waiting until she followed suit.

This felt a lot better to Jennifer.

She looked at him and did her best to superimpose *the friend she was seeing* over *the hunky semi-naked man who had scrambled her brains*.

She sighed and then said honestly, 'It was bloody stressful, now that you ask.'

'Tell me about it.'

Jennifer sat on the sofa, swivelled to face him and then drew her knees up and crossed her legs.

'Put it this way. I figured I would rather have been in your shoes talking business with Roberto, and I don't even know how to talk business. She asked me loads of questions about…about *us*. She wanted to talk about feelings and love and when we first realised that we were destined for one another.'

'Sounds a bit of a nightmare,' Gabriel agreed, 'but I'm guessing you swatted away the questions and ducked behind vague answers?'

'What else could I do? Gabriel, she's really invested in a future between us. She's practically planning the wedding. By the end of the week, she'll have picked names for the grandkids.'

'Did you give her any reason to think that there might be one or two hurdles along the way?'

'I tried. I said one or two things about your workaholic tendencies and jet-setting lifestyle, but she wasn't having it. Opposites attract, she said, along with *birds of a feather.* I think she was going for both options just in case. I'm surprised she didn't throw in the one about absence making the heart grow fonder.'

'Don't worry. Once this week is done and dusted and life gets back into its usual routine, she'll begin to see the cracks.'

'Maybe.'

'At any rate, it's too late to do anything but play a wait-and-see game. Fact is, though, her mental health is getting better and better by the day. She actually used that high-end mobile phone I bought for her two months ago and sent me some pictures of the town you visited today. I thought she'd stuck the damned thing in a drawer and forgotten about it.'

'I'm beginning to think that your mum might be a lot shrewder than either of us imagines.' Jennifer sighed. 'I mean, you must get that calculating streak in you from someone.'

'Yes, but perhaps not my mother. My father was essentially a good-looking conman, the sort of bastard who comes for dinner, sizes up your house and leaves with the silver cutlery. Some of us might call that calculating.'

They looked at one another, and she flushed. There had been that hardness, an underlying edge she'd heard before as though he'd allowed her to see a secret part of himself, but only for a moment.

'What makes you say that, anyway? About my mum being calculating?' he prodded with a frown.

'Maybe *calculating* is the wrong term.' She gazed at him for a fleeting second. He was so complex. There were hidden depths to him that existed beneath the surface, and she itched to find them with a burning curiosity she'd never felt before. 'Maybe it's shrewdness laced with a lot of tenderness and affection, but…it's just a feeling. She said, out of the blue, that everyone has second thoughts when it comes to relationships, but she knows that even if I do, I shouldn't be swayed by that, because you and I are right for one another. Almost as if she was trying to pre-empt me from finding reasons to walk away.'

'Doesn't every mother give that *second thoughts* speech?'

'Only on the day you're supposed to get married, when she finds you staring out a window and contemplating whether you can jump through it just in case you've made a mistake. The speech doesn't tend to happen three seconds into a supposed fledgling relationship.'

'When it comes to my mother's levels of shrewdness, there's a limit to what she can do.' Gabriel stood up and looked at her with a remote, guarded expression. 'With the best will in the world, I don't think she'll be able to manacle our wrists together and frog-march us up the aisle.'

'No.' Jennifer hesitated. She could feel something in the air between them, a pulsing electric charge that made her feel as though making conversation, usually so effortless, was now like wading through treacle. 'Gabriel, is something wrong?'

'Wrong? What do you mean by that? What do you mean by *wrong*?'

'See, *that's* what I mean.'

She glared at him, annoyed because he was being obtuse and annoyed that she wasn't sure whether it was deliberate or not. This uncomfortable argument, and she wasn't sure whether it was even an argument, was so unlike them.

'Not following you.' Gabriel's dark eyes were suddenly wary and distant.

'Your attitude!' she exclaimed helplessly. Even as she stared at him, she could feel an unnerving physical response to a masculinity that she had never quite allowed to penetrate her consciousness. 'Look.' She steadied her voice and tried a smile on for size, but his expression didn't soften. 'Have I done something to upset you, Gabriel?' She drew in a deep breath and went for it. 'I know this is an unusual situation, and…ah…we're not accustomed to…' she nodded around her, but her eyes remained on his face '…these living arrangements, but… you *did* say that sharing this space had one or two advantages. Didn't you? That we could relax here away from watchful eyes and be ourselves except…except *we're not being ourselves, are we*?'

A thick silence greeted this.

'Yes, I did say that,' Gabriel admitted gruffly. He slanted her the shadow of a smile whilst choosing to ignore what she'd said about the subtle change in their interactions. 'There are definite advantages to being stuck here on our own, but maybe…'

'Maybe what?'

Gabriel looked at her levelly. Should he admit to concerns about them sharing this place? And if he did, what exactly would those concerns be that he would admit? That he was alarmed at the way he was finding it difficult to take his eyes off her? Especially since that little encounter in the kitchen?

Nope. That wasn't going to do. He didn't know where this sudden loss of self-control was coming from, but he was going to nip it in the bud to stop it having a little fun at the expense of his good judgement, which had never let him down before.

'Maybe we should cut this stay short,' he abruptly offered. 'No need to remain here for another week. I have perhaps a couple of days' worth of work, and then we can feasibly make an excuse to return to England.'

'Would that be okay with your mum? It would be a shame when you look at how well she's doing here, and it's only been a day or so! She's really taken to Luisa and Roberto. Perhaps because they don't know her back story. Maybe it's like starting a clean chapter. They don't feel sorry for her the way some of her friends back home probably would, so she feels she can be herself, be vulnerable after everything she's been through, without eliciting well-meaning pity. She's very proud.'

'One day,' Gabriel mused in a roughened undertone, 'you're going to make some lucky guy a very good wife.'

'What do you mean?'

'Exactly what I just said.' Gabriel felt that this was the time to kill off the onset of whatever weird attraction had suddenly started gripping him. He needed to clear his head and, within himself, re-establish his boundaries. She was fine. He, annoyingly, wasn't. If he verbalised the route his mind should be taking, then his body might get the hint and pay attention.

'Look at you,' he murmured with heartfelt sincerity. 'You never wanted to do this, to be here, but here you are. Even now that I've given you the chance to cut things short, you still have my mother's welfare in mind.' He paused. 'I appreciate that. You're one of a kind, Jen.'

'Thank you.'

'I mean it.' He slanted her a crooked smile and gritted his teeth against the temptation to keep staring. 'You're thoughtful and considerate and always willing to put other people ahead of yourself.'

'Thanks again, Gabriel. I had no idea you thought I was in line for a sainthood, although I'm really not that person.'

'Oh, but you are, which is why you're meant for marriage to a good guy, a guy who will appreciate you.' He laughed self-deprecatingly. 'I, on the other hand, am perfectly cut out for a hard-as-nails woman.'

'Why do you say that?'

'You know why, surely. After the example my father set? Crash course in why love and marriage aren't for me. Lots of people might come from a broken background and continue, against the odds, to actually believe that wishing on a star and hoping love works out are enough, but fortunately not me.' He thought about the pain of finding his dad only to be turned away, sent packing, shown the cruel face of parental indifference. Hope, like love, equalled pain and loss. 'Although I might have to ask you to give her a few vital pointers on making my mother happy.'

'Or,' Jennifer responded with a tight smile, rising to her feet and concluding a conversation that felt vaguely offensive even though it obviously wasn't, 'you could try casting your net a little wider and going for someone who's less interested in taking and more interested in giving. That might do the trick, and then you wouldn't have to depend on someone to give any lessons on *how to be a decent human being.* What are the plans for this evening? Will Luisa and Roberto be joining us somewhere for dinner? Or will it just be the three of us?'

Tension hung in the air, but Gabriel welcomed it. He felt he could deal with a little tension a lot better than he could deal with whatever was screwing with his libido and firing up his imagination.

'Luisa has helped the chef to prepare some homemade pasta for us, or maybe I should say that Luisa has given orders to the chef on how to prepare pasta the way she likes it. Roberto confided that she doesn't think anyone can make pasta the way she can, and she's determined to show us just how good she is. Also, I'm assuming my mother is pretty exhausted after today's activities?'

Back in control of his wayward thoughts and perversely pleased to have got under her skin, Gabriel watched her with brooding intensity.

She was pink-faced and ruffled and hot after her sightseeing trip. Her clothes, which were loose and unrevealing, nevertheless clung to her curves, to her rounded hips, her breasts, her long legs.

He tightened his jaw.

'Think I'll remove myself to the office to catch up on some work,' he said tersely. 'Give you time to use the bathroom, have a shower, freshen up. Mind if I meet you at Roberto's in a couple of hours?'

'Of course not.'

'And one other thing which only occurred to me when I was on vineyard inspection today… If we're sharing this cottage, it might help if there's some semblance of us sharing the bedroom. My mother is sure to wander over at some point, and she might be a little astonished if we're sleeping in separate bedrooms.'

'I hadn't thought about that.'

She hadn't. She'd been so consumed with the business of trying to get her act together that small details like that had ended up in her blind spot.

Jennifer thought about her personal belongings nestling alongside his and felt a slow burn spread through her. He was already on the move. She could see that from the way he was looking away from her, his mind on thoughts of work, she assumed. He'd tossed that observation at her and had no idea of the reaction it had evoked.

'What do you suggest?' she asked.

Their eyes met, and he tilted his head to one side thoughtfully. 'Doesn't have to be dramatic. No need to move in lock, stock and smoking barrel. A few items of clothing draped here and there, and of course make sure your bed is made with hospital corners so that there's some pretence at us actually being what we're supposed to be. Two people who share a bed. She might be old-fashioned, but I don't think the twenty-first century has completely passed her by. I doubt she'll get it into her head to pop in for a quick chat and then suddenly decide to go through the entire cottage forensically for signs of anything that might not add up, but we should probably work on a *better safe than sorry* basis.'

'Okay. I'll do some draping before I head over, shall I?'

'Drape away. I'll be in the office with the door shut, and I'll see you in a couple of hours.'

'Gabriel…'

He was already moving towards the office, leaving her to do her own thing, but he paused and glanced over his shoulder to her with a questioning look.

A *politely* questioning look.

'Yes?'

You're not the same... What's wrong...? Was it such an unpleasant shock seeing me in my pyjamas...?

'Nothing. I'll see you later.'

Gabriel had a quick check of the cottage before he headed over to join his mother, Jennifer and their hosts.

He emerged from the office, knowing that she'd left half an hour previously, to find that she had indeed strategically left some shoes on the floor of his bedroom and a couple of T-shirts neatly folded on the chest of drawers.

If his mother did pop in, she wouldn't be shocked to find that they had spread their belongings out in the cottage. Why not? Why cram belongings into one wardrobe when two were available?

He doubted she would be that thorough, though.

He paused for a few seconds when he was in the bedroom Jennifer had chosen and noted that the bed looked as fresh as when they'd arrived. Unslept in. His eyes lingered, and his mind played with tantalising images of her in the undisturbed-looking bed. In those pyjamas.

He impatiently killed that thought stone dead and headed towards the main house.

It was a little after seven. The shadows were beginning to creep in. The vast expanse of vineyards was bathed in mellow, golden hues. The last of the sun lit up the squat cobbled stone walls that crisscrossed through the vineyards and disappeared behind the tall, imposing silhouettes of the cypress trees. Outside the house, there were lanterns strung above the wide patio that circled the building. They swayed in the evening breeze.

The problem of his disobedient libido was still on Gabriel's mind as he hesitated for a few seconds outside the front door, hand poised to knock.

How to deal with that?

Fighting it certainly wasn't the way forward. The more he fought what his body was doing, the more the temptation of the forbidden beckoned. Bring things back down to Planet Normal and discomforting reactions would disappear.

He was forgetting the banal reality of their situation. She was there, pretending to be his lover for the sake of his mother's mental and physical well-being.

It was a job. A business transaction. For which he was paying her! Even if that had been at his own insistence.

He would go in there, wholeheartedly commit to the pretence of having a relationship, and re-establish common sense. This restless, edgy, unexplained attraction would be put back in its box, never to make another appearance.

Spirits duly lifted, Gabriel knocked, was let in by one of the people he had contracted for the time they were there to help out, and was shown to the sitting room.

Jennifer heard Gabriel's approach before he was at the door, the hairs on her arm feathering as if some sixth sense she'd never known she possessed was suddenly in play. She instantly tensed. She was sitting with her back to the door and a glass of chianti in her hand as she chatted away with Roberto about wine production.

On the sofa opposite, Francesca and Luisa were huddled, talking like old friends. Looking at them, Jennifer could understand why she and Gabriel were doing what they were doing.

She had spent the best part of an hour with Francesca before they had joined Luisa and Roberto, and Francesca was happy. Her cheeks were pink. Her eyes were glowing. She wasn't at all tired from their day out sightseeing. It was more than just the fact that Gabriel was supposedly on the cusp of settling down with someone she loved, although that played a great part in it.

It was also being here, away from reminders of her mortality, away from a social life she had more or less abandoned, and away from all her doubts and daily anxieties.

Jennifer was sure Francesca would return to England a changed woman, so perhaps Gabriel had been right all along. Once his mum's head was back in the right place, she would be able to deal with the disappointment of her son's supposed happy-ever-after story hitting the buffers.

She was aware of Gabriel's presence behind her seconds before she felt the weight of his hand on her shoulder. It rested on her in a gentle caress. Then he leaned down, and his breath was on her cheek as he dropped a light kiss on the side of her neck.

Her eyes widened. In passing, she noticed the way Francesca and Luisa were tickled pink by the caress, the way Roberto nodded approvingly. Mostly, though, she was too busy going bright red and trying to harness her scattered thoughts to do much but continue to redden.

'Had a good day, my darling?' he crooned. Eventually Jennifer glanced at him, half twisting in the chair just as he straightened and pulled a chair right next to hers. Then he shifted it a little bit more so that their knees were touching. Glancing down, her mouth went dry at the sight of muscular thighs stretched against the fine linen of his trousers.

She hurriedly lifted her gaze to the amused curve of his mouth and then to the dark eyes, shielded by impossibly long sooty lashes.

'Already told you…er…darling…we had a fabulous

day. Isn't that right, Francesca? Fabulous day sightseeing?' She licked her lips when he squeezed her knee and then let his hand remain there, burning a hole through her summery dress. When he casually slid it a tiny bit under the hem of the dress, she felt her body go up in flames.

Her eyes glazed over. Francesca, on cue, had launched into an enthusiastic account of the day. Jennifer half listened and steadfastly kept her eyes fixed anywhere but on the man wreaking havoc on her nervous system.

For the entire evening.

They stood as they were called to the table for dinner…and his arm was slung over her shoulder.

They sat at the table…and his eyes, she could feel, were riveted to her profile as if he were in the presence of the most fascinating woman on the planet.

She joined in the conversation, and his hand would briefly linger over hers in a gentle caress…

She asked for the salt, and he would solicitously look up at her and then meet her eyes for a soulful few seconds before handing it over.

What was he playing at?

Of course, she knew. This was the loving couple image they had both signed up for, including her. Everything was phoney, unreal, *a lie.* Suddenly they weren't friends any longer, not the friends they'd always been.

She was playing a part and so was he, and somehow their friendship had become lost in the process.

She contained her misery through the course of the evening, hid it under a smile. She made sure to chat and laugh in all the right places even though she was painfully conscious of a tightening knot in the pit of her stomach at the thought of how things were changing between her and Gabriel.

Would things return to being normal and *real* between them when this was over?

Francesca was the first to retire, immediately after dessert. With relief, Gabriel took the lead and politely declined after-dinner drinks with their hosts.

'Another busy day tomorrow,' he said, moving towards the door and taking her with him, fingers lovingly linked. 'I'm visiting a couple of other vineyards to see production methods.'

'And will competitors be willing to show you how it's done? Seems awfully generous,' Jennifer remarked, inserting herself into the conversation whilst simultaneously slipping out of his suffocating, heart-stopping casual embrace.

Their eyes met. 'You'd be shocked at the power of charm and persuasion,' Gabriel replied with the sort of silky self-assurance she had become accustomed to over the years. 'I've already started building my contacts and working out how we can all benefit one another. Like one big, happy family. Working together is always better than trying to go it alone,' he added expansively.

Jennifer snorted, and he grinned. Just for a second, they were back to the place she knew and loved. But then, as soon as they were outside, his hand dropped. She could feel the remoteness between them again.

She pulled away and then swept past him as soon as he opened the door to the cottage, but she didn't fly towards her bedroom even though she wanted badly to.

Instead, she spun round, arms folded, and looked at him with simmering fury.

'You're being weird!'

'What? I'm *being weird*? How am I *being weird*?'

Gabriel looked at her with equal fury, but he knew that his fury wasn't with her. It was with himself. He was furious that he'd spent the evening playing a part, in the hope that it would remind him that this was all it was… the touching, the looking. *A part.*

But he had still felt his body reacting, stirring, responding, and now…

God, she was so beautiful. He'd never seen her furious with him, and the sight was something spectacular to behold. Fiery. Fierce. He clenched his jaw and didn't respond for a couple of seconds.

'Well?'

He'd lowered his head, but now he looked up to see that she had taken a few steps closer to him. In that moment…

In that moment, nothing mattered—not common sense, not self-control, not reason.

Temptation played its trump card. He moved towards her so that their bodies were inches apart. He could feel the heat emanating from her, could breathe in whatever perfume she was wearing, could see the clear, dramatic blue of her eyes and the soft curve of her full mouth.

'Want to know what's bugging me?' he growled. 'You, Jen. *You're* bugging me, and want to know why?'

Oh, yes…she wanted to know why. He could see it in the widening of her eyes and the way her breathing stilled.

She wanted him. She wanted him just as much as he wanted her. She wasn't backing away at speed from the bold challenge in his eyes. She was coming towards it, like a moth to a flame, whether she was aware of that or not.

'Ha,' she said weakly. 'I have no idea what you mean.'

'Would you like to find out?'

The answer was right there in the slow colour crawling into her cheeks, in the parting of her lips, in the wide dilation of her pupils.

'Let me show you,' he growled.

He curled his hand into his hair, pulled her towards him and then lowered his head and kissed her.

CHAPTER SEVEN

SHOCK SWAMPED HER as those cool, firm lips met hers. It didn't last long, and was immediately replaced by a soaring feeling that this was the moment she'd been waiting for.

It made *no sense*. He was wrong, wrong, *wrong*, and she should be pulling back, putting an ocean of clear blue water between them…

But instead, she leaned into him and wrapped her arms around his neck and pulled him closer, returning the kiss with hot urgency. Their tongues meshed, and Jennifer stifled a moan of pure pleasure. She half groaned into his mouth because she didn't want to break the wild, electric connection between them.

And his mouth wasn't enough. She wanted more of him to touch more of her.

She clicked her tongue in aching frustration when he pulled back and looked at her, their eyes meeting. His hand was still curled into her hair, and their bodies were so closely pressed together that it would have been a stretch to slide a sheet of paper between them.

'Jen…' he muttered huskily, but he wasn't pulling back, and the curled fist in her hair loosened as he gently pushed her hair back and kept his hand there in a softly caressing gesture.

'I know,' she breathed. She had to stop herself from reaching up to touch his face. She knew him so well, and yet now, in this moment, there was still so much more to discover.

'I didn't mean for this to happen. Hell, Jen…my self-control is usually rock-solid.'

'Hmm, it's a bad idea,' she dutifully breathed, but she still wanted to touch him, and as he wasn't pulling back, she guessed that he felt the same way.

But it *was* a bad idea. Terrible idea, in fact. They were friends, and nowhere was this kiss in the friendship landscape. It was nothing, meant *nothing*. She would make sure of that, because she wanted everything he could never give.

And yet…

'Just terrible,' she added earnestly for good measure.

'It's essential,' he murmured, sifting his fingers through her hair and lightly stroking the back of her neck, 'that we walk away from whatever the hell this is and forget it ever happened.'

'For sure. Although, Gabriel…'

'Talk to me.'

'I know that's what we should do,' Jennifer said roughly, 'but…'

'Think before you say anything else,' he muttered. 'I'm in a place I never expected to be and have never been before, so I…for the first time in my life, I…'

'You what?'

'I can't predict the outcome.'

'And is that such a bad thing?'

'For me? Yes.'

'Got it,' Jennifer agreed, thinking that this was definitely one of those surprises best avoided at all costs. She sighed and curved into his soft caress, then craned up to lick his chin, the corner of his mouth…

She didn't get any further.

With a guttural, stifled oath of abandonment, Gabriel swept her off her feet and was carrying her towards his bedroom. She leaned back with her hair tumbling in a wavy cascade, swinging, as he kicked open the door and deposited her on the bed.

The windows were open and the shutters flung back, allowing in the soft, silvery glow of the moonlight.

The delicate beams of light silhouetted Gabriel as he stood by the side of the bed for a few seconds. Jennifer wondered whether he was having second thoughts.

She knew that she should have been. She should, right now, be horrified and mortified. Frankly, right now, she shouldn't be here at all, lying in his bed, fully clothed and waiting for what felt inevitable.

Her heart stopped as he began to undress.

She propped herself up on one elbow and stared in the barely there light. His movements were slow and deliberate, and he never took his eyes off her face.

'Enjoying the view?' he asked with rampant amusement.

'It's not bad.'

'Very hurtful.'

Looking at her propped up like that with all her tumbling dark hair and sexy curves, Gabriel felt, weirdly, *at peace*.

The relationship they'd always had, the friendship

he'd always cherished, should have made this awkward, but for some reason, it felt natural.

Was this the allure of a friends-with-benefits situation? He'd never, not once, contemplated the viability of any such relationship, yet here he was, and yes…*it felt natural.*

He wondered whether it was the freedom of knowing that he was with a woman who understood him and where he was coming from.

Jennifer had no expectations of him. She wasn't looking for love and commitment. She knew where he stood on that. She could him give her body, but her heart would be safe from him.

Was that why he felt so liberated, standing here in front of her lazily curious gaze?

Liberated and turned on in a way he had never felt before.

He was barely aware of his shirt hitting the ground because she was the only thing filling his head, suffocating every feeling but the overwhelming one of craving.

He moved towards the window and closed the shutters. Suddenly the moonlight was snuffed out, and his eyes had to adjust to the sudden blackness.

'Your turn,' he commanded huskily when he was once more towering by the side of the bed, staring down at her.

Jennifer slid off the bed and stood right by him, shorter than him but only by a few inches. She gazed up at him, hands trembling with what he hoped was a mixture of nerves and simmering excitement.

'On second thought,' he said shakily, 'I want to do the honours.'

He reached for her hands and held them in his. Before he began to undress her, he lowered his head and kissed her again. This time, the kiss was long and lingering and sweetly, deliciously thorough.

He felt her soft sigh like a caress.

'Sure about this, Jen?'

'Never been more sure about anything in my life.'

'Even though it makes no sense?'

'I'm going with the flow.'

'Well, at least you don't come with any illusions,' he said with heartfelt sincerity.

'At least I don't,' she agreed, kissing him now on the side of his neck, licking him and tasting the saltiness of his skin. 'And stop with the talking…'

'Your wish, my command.'

He undressed her. Bit by slow bit, and with every small revelation of naked skin, he became more and more turned on. When she was finally standing in front of him in her bra and panties, he ran his hands over her smooth shoulders and along her arms, like a blind man wanting to commit to memory every small inch of her glorious body.

'You're beautiful, Jennifer,' he husked.

'That's sweet of you, Gabriel, but honestly, not necessary.'

'What do you mean?'

He moved to run exploring hands along her sides, along her waist, allowing himself to savour the anticipation of touching more…her breasts, her legs and what beckoned between them.

'You don't have to do the whole compliment thing.'

Gabriel pulled back and frowned. 'The whole compliment thing?'

'The chat-up lines, you know.'

'You *are* beautiful, Jen.' He began kissing her again, pulling away to say in little tender bursts, 'and…' a flick of his tongue against her mouth '… I do not…' a sexy breath in her ear and the dart of his tongue to accompany it '…do chat-up lines.' He pulled back, but he was grinning. 'You make me sound superficial.'

'Far be it from me to do that.'

'One thing I never do is lie. If I tell you that you're beautiful, then you're beautiful. You're beautiful.'

'Says the man who's managed to lure me into pretending to be involved with him for the sake of his mother.'

'Touché, but that was a little white lie,' Gabriel corrected her. 'Spoken with the best of intentions. Besides, it's not so much a lie now, wouldn't you agree? And what was it you said about enough talking…?'

He tugged the straps of her cotton bra, inched them down and gazed, barely able to breathe, at her breasts as they were oh so slowly revealed.

He'd died and gone to Heaven.

His hands were shaking when the bra was finally off, unclasped and on the ground with the rest of her discarded clothes. He cupped her abundant breasts in his hands. His hands were big, but they still didn't manage to contain her breasts completely. He rolled his thumbs over the tips of the big circular discs of her nipples and groaned.

His erection was pushing against his boxers like a rod of steel.

Still kissing her, he removed one hand from her breast

and guided it towards his erection. Then he had to grit his teeth and contain his urgent desire to go further and faster as her hand circled his length through the light cotton.

'Okay, not sure how much more I can stand of this,' he groaned. He got rid of the boxers at speed and propelled her back towards the bed and they both half fell onto the mattress in a tumult of moans and stifled gasps and low laughter.

In her head, Jennifer couldn't have agreed more. She was so wet that she could feel her thighs sliding against one another, and Lord…the feel of him, of that massive erection, throbbing in her hand.

She'd never experienced anything like the rush of blinding desire that had engulfed her.

She could barely manage to free herself of her underwear, was barely aware of him sinking onto her, as naked as she was. She felt the hardness of him between her thighs, nudging as she opened her legs to him. He knew just how to press against her, to rub and slide against the nub of her clitoris until she was going crazy with wanting more.

She held his hips still for a couple of seconds. Her eyelids fluttered. She arched up as he began to tenderly kiss her. He peppered her face with kisses, lingered on her mouth, but not for long.

She knew just how he was going to explore her body, and she couldn't wait. Her brain just seemed to stop working altogether as the lips that had been on hers travelled lazily down to her collarbone, licking and nipping before settling on one nipple.

She felt him relax into the job at hand as he began to suckle. He drew her nipple into his mouth and circled it with his tongue, and her whole body arched up so that the sensation could be amplified. She curled her fingers into his dark hair, spread her legs wide open beneath him and abandoned herself to what was happening to her body.

Physically they seemed the perfect match. Was that why she was so comfortable doing this with him, even though every logical brain cell in her head was screaming out that she was crossing a dangerous divide?

She bucked and moaned as he continued to lave her nipple with his tongue, first one then the other, taking his time. She could barely take any more. Then he slowly trailed his hand over her rib cage and along her stomach. It was a light, feathery touch, but it moved on an inexorable path towards the wetness at her core.

He edged himself off her, and his mouth replaced his hand. Jennifer shuddered convulsively. Anticipation built higher and higher to the breaking point as he moved to position himself between her legs. When he gently parted her womanhood, she was on the point of exploding.

And yet she could scarcely breathe. She was as tense as a bowstring yet softly open to receive his questing mouth.

She tensed when his tongue flicked and found the tight bud of her clitoris.

She opened drowsy eyes and looked down at his dark head as it moved between her thighs. The sight was so erotic that for a few seconds, she found herself holding her breath. She closed her eyes, shielded her face in the crook of her arm and let herself move to the rhythm of his tongue as it continued to tease and flick and lick.

He wasn't going to stop. He was going to take her over the edge, and she wanted that. She couldn't have made herself stop even if she'd wanted to as the surge of hot passion inside her rose to unstoppable levels.

She cried out as an orgasm tore through her. She arched up against his mouth as her body spasmed uncontrollably. On and on it seemed to go, and she was as weak as a kitten when she gradually came down from a high she had never experienced.

'I should have waited,' she apologised when he'd straightened to lie next to her. 'I'm not too sorry, though, because that was amazing.'

He manoeuvred her so that they were facing one another and smiled.

'Quite the compliment.'

'Don't let it go to your head, Gabriel.' But she smiled back, pulled him against her and kissed the side of his mouth.

'I liked it as well,' he murmured. 'I liked seeing you lose control like that.'

'Now it's your turn…' She reached down without taking her eyes off him and began to tease, building up a slow, steady rhythm and watching with satisfaction as he clenched his jaw against losing himself too fast in the pleasure of what she was doing. When he tried to slow her down, she laughed softly and brushed his hand aside.

But he had ultimate control, even when she replaced her hand with her mouth, even when she positioned herself so that they were mutually pleasuring one another, when her body was raring to go again, aching to reach that place it had just visited.

The flick of his tongue on her as she tasted him was almost too much.

She squirmed off him but then stayed him when he began moving to get protection.

'I'm on the pill,' she said, 'and it's not because I'm all over the place on a thousand different dates, in a quest for Mr Right. I'm not. It's to regulate my periods.'

'That's a lot of information,' Gabriel responded, and he thought two things at once. The first was that he trusted her when she said that she was using contraception. If any other woman had said the very same thing, he would still have donned his own, because he was a very rich man and *who knew*?

The second was that, deep in a part of him he barely acknowledged, he was glad that she didn't play the field. He never thought she had, but to hear her say it in that suddenly shy, stilted voice made something in him soar with unexplained pleasure.

He kissed her softly, tenderly, and this time they made love with less desperation but no less urgency.

He tried to go as slowly as possible, and he succeeded, but only just. As he thrust into her, felt the tightness of her around him without the barrier of a condom, it was all he could do to maintain control. He moved gently at first, patiently waiting for her rhythm to match his. Then he deepened and quickened his movements until there was nothing left inside him but the blinding roar of pleasure pulsing through his veins. It exploded in something so wonderful, so powerful that he was utterly spent when he half collapsed onto her before rolling off to close his eyes, at last, for a few seconds.

They were both spent. Her body next to his was as hot and sweaty as his was, and lying in the darkness, staring up at the ceiling, he could feel her doing the same, staring up in the quiet room, waiting for a conversation to be had.

'Well, that was very nice.' She was the first to break the silence, turning onto her side and propping herself up on one elbow.

Gabriel relaxed and smiled without turning immediately to face her, just feeling a wave of relief that there was no awkwardness there. She wasn't about to embark on a soul-searching conversation about the ramifications of what they'd both done.

He rolled so that they were both facing one another.

'Very nice?' he queried. 'Can we do better than that?'

'Nine out of ten.'

'What accounts for the missing point?'

'What accounts for the missing point,' Jennifer said gravely, 'is that ten out of ten would mean perfection, and there's no such thing as perfection. That's something I always tell my pupils.'

Lying there next to him, Jennifer heard the light teasing in her voice and knew, instinctively, that this was the right approach to what had just happened.

Inside there was a tumult of emotions swirling around, destabilising, confusing, disturbing emotions. Those would have to be dealt with later, in the privacy of her own bedroom, where she could inspect them and pick them apart and then try and put them back together in a way that made sense.

Right now, it was important to remember that what was destabilising and confusing and disturbing *for her* would not be the same for Gabriel.

He was a man of the world. This would be unexpected for him, but at the end of the day, he wouldn't be torn apart with conflicting emotions and would certainly not be interested in handling an agonising question and answer session about what had just happened between them.

She, on the other hand, whilst having dated any number of guys, was remarkably green round the ears when it came to sex. It was a big deal for her. Huge.

Keep things light, she decided now. Be the adult he thought he was, even though she knew differently. The important thing to take away was that this was lust, and lust had an end date.

Make things weird and uncomfortable and it would be the end of their friendship.

'So…' She circled his bare chest with her finger and then flicked her eyes to him. 'You know what I'm going to say next, don't you?'

She could almost feel him stiffen. Did he think that she would suddenly turn into the sort of clingy woman who might try to pin him down just because they'd slept together?

She was here because he thought she knew the score, and the score didn't involve clinginess.

'What?' he asked.

'Mistakes happen,' she returned, cool, composed and

controlled. She shrugged. 'I say we move on and chalk it down as a good old-fashioned one-night holiday stand.'

This, Gabriel thought, was exactly what he wanted to hear. A one-night stand. Atmosphere getting the better of them. Two consenting adults giving in to temptation. It happened.

'A one-night stand?' he echoed with a frown.

'Absolutely.' She began easing herself off the bed while Gabriel watched in mounting dissatisfaction.

'Wait. Where are you going?'

'Back to my bedroom.'

'Why?'

'What do you mean, *why*? Because it's where I sleep?'

'Come back to bed,' he said gruffly.

'Gabriel, we both know that this should never have happened, but it did, and there's no point talking about it. We…you're…we're friends, not…'

'Lovers? Funny, but that's not what my body's telling me. Is that what your body's telling you? That we're just friends?'

'I'm not talking about this.'

'Come back to bed.'

'Why? Why?'

'Because I still want you.'

The roughly spoken words hung in the air between them, shimmering, alluring and dangerous.

Gabriel looked at her in brooding silence. He wanted to snatch her up, hold her close and settle her right back in his bed, next to him, and he had no idea where that urge was coming from. When it came to women, he always travelled light. Jennifer was a lot more than any other woman, but even so…

'This isn't about want.'

'I can't focus when you're standing there trying to find your clothes. I want to make love to you all over again.'

Jennifer felt the dampness between her legs again as her mind filled with erotic images, as she remembered the lightness of his touch on her and the way her body had responded.

He wanted her, and just the way he'd said that, his voice low and demanding and husky and unsteady…

She'd tried to lock forbidden thoughts back in their box, but now the lid was open, and they were everywhere. Her eyelids fluttered, and she drew in a shaky breath.

'You're being a spoiled brat, Gabriel.'

'I know. Come back to bed and tell me all about it.'

She shot him a jaundiced, frustrated, impatient look, but he was patting the space next to him on the bed, and she so desperately wanted to return to occupy that space.

Plus, she was feeling a little ridiculous standing there, clutching some of her clothes, completely naked in front of his lazy, hungry gaze.

But mostly, she just wanted him so badly, still.

'I'm not… Okay, I will, but that doesn't mean that we're going to…to…'

'To…? To…? To make sweet, sweet love until we're too tired to carry on? To turn each other on until we can't think? To do that sort of thing over and over again?'

'Stop it, Gabriel,' she whispered, but her legs were

propelling her back to the bed. She sighed with pleasure when she was nestled back next to him, when she could feel the hardness of his body against hers, and then his arm came around her, drawing her close.

'This just isn't on,' she said shakily, placing the flat of her hand against his chest and feeling the steady beat of his heart.

'But it's not a mistake, Jen, and I don't think it's something we can walk away from and pretend never took place. It happened, and we'll have a conversation about what we do about it. And what I'd like to do about it is to carry on. It's not as though we're not practically engaged to be married.'

'This isn't funny.'

'I know it's not, but just think about the alternative…'

'You mean—' she tilted her face so that she was looking at him, her blue eyes serious '—the sensible one where we put this behind us?'

'The very one,' he murmured. 'If we try to pretend we never made love, don't you think that every time we look at one another, all we'll be able to see is the elephant in the room? Do you have any idea how impossible it will be for us to return to the place we left behind? To enjoy the friendship we once had? There would be too much unfinished business between us. We'd never survive it.'

'Don't say that.'

'Logically, I know we shouldn't have done what we did, but my body doesn't agree. My body is telling me that making love with you was mind-blowing, and I don't regret a second of it. Do you? Have any regrets? Regrets that aren't tied up with common sense? Tell me the absolute truth, Jen. If you do, then I'll walk away and do what you ask, pretend it never happened. If you really think you could live with that, then say so.'

His words carved an inexorable path through her. She thought about what he'd said. She thought about seeing him, knowing that they'd made love, wanting more yet existing in a constant state of permanent, agonising denial. What would they talk about when they were alone together? Would they end up in stilted silence, searching around for things to say, knowing that what was unspoken was hovering in the air between them?

Why was she so scared? She would never, ever completely lose herself in this man. Knowing him as well as she did had its advantages! She would never, *could never*, compromise her heart with any guy who was a commitment-phobe.

She balled her open hand into a soft fist and tapped it helplessly against his chest.

'I don't regret it,' she murmured on a helpless sigh. 'I enjoyed it.'

'I know.'

'You're so cocky, Gabriel Garcia.'

'Only with you.'

'Is that so?'

He didn't answer. His kissed her slowly and felt her melt in his arms. The rush of satisfaction was so intense it knocked him for six. How many times could one man make love in a night? Countless, it would seem, because he could feel the stirring of his erection as it began to push against her.

'We'll eventually exhaust one another, Jen, trust me.'

'Of course we will. I know that.' She parted her legs

and let him rub his hardness against her, luxuriating in the way he was pleasuring her. She closed her eyes and held on to his shoulders. For a couple of seconds, he lost himself in the sensation of simply watching her.

'And when that happens,' he heard himself continue, 'all this will be behind us.'

'I know. Why are you still talking?'

Gabriel had no idea, because this kind of chat usually left him cold. He was driven to conclude something, some line of thought that needed to be slotted into place.

He laughed sheepishly and edged back so that he could look at her. Her cheeks were flushed, her mouth parted and her eyes were drowsy with desire.

At this point, turned on as he was, there should have been no words, no conversation. Right now he should have been doing what he wanted to do instead of…talking.

'Good question,' he admitted. 'Maybe I'm turning into one of those sensitive types who writes poetry and hugs trees.'

'Now wouldn't that be a turn-up for the books?'

'I just want to make sure that you're on board with all of this. I know…' What did he know? He was the one doing the talking… She seemed perfectly fine with their decision after a little hesitation. Since when was he a guy who wanted to analyse situations that required no analysis? 'I know,' he continued heavily, 'that this isn't your kind of thing, sleeping with a man when there's no prospect of it going in the direction you might want. I just don't want you to…well, to get hurt. I'm experienced. I can handle this situation—'

'Oh, for goodness' sake, Gabriel!' She clicked her tongue impatiently and rolled her eyes. 'All these warnings! I wouldn't be here if I didn't want to be here or if I thought I was going to get hurt. Why would I? Who wants to start something if they know they're going to be hurt at the end of it? You're right. We need to…get this fever out of our system, for want of a better way of putting it. And once we do, it'll be just as if we've caught a bug and got over it. When that happens, we'll tell your mum that it's all over, and we won't be lying. It'll genuinely be over, and we'll return to being the friends we've always been.'

CHAPTER EIGHT

'I FEEL TERRIBLE, GABRIEL. Do you feel terrible?' Jennifer wasn't looking at him. She was sitting contentedly in a chair outside one of the many piazzas in the charming town they had decided to visit for the day. She was happily working her way through a gelato with Gabriel right next to her, both of them facing out to people-watch while they chatted.

'I can't say I'm feeling particularly terrible at the moment.'

'It's the third day we've abandoned your mother to do our own thing.'

'I prefer to think that it's the third day she's hustled us out of the house because she doesn't want to get in the way of the lovebirds having a good time.'

They were lovebirds. In a manner of speaking.

That was how Jennifer felt, and if she occasionally had one or two qualms that she might just be getting in out of her depth, then she very quickly stifled those qualms. Really things were utterly straightforward.

They would continue with what they had, would wait for this fever to pass. In the meantime, they'd enjoy one another. Not a string attached in sight!

'How else do we deal with this thing between us?' he

had murmured a couple of nights before, when they'd been lying in each other's arms, spent and with the light of a silvery moon casting shadows over their bodies on the bed. 'I'm happy, you're happy, my mother is happy. All one big, happy family.'

Jennifer had been more than willing to go along with that conclusion. She was having fun. She'd always thought that she was someone who enjoyed life, but never like this.

When had she ever sat in a piazza, in a town perched on a hilltop where, from one of the many towers, you could see rolling vineyards, olive groves and fields that stretched towards a limitless horizon, drenched in sunshine?

She reached out her hand, felt for his and linked their fingers.

She sneaked a sideways glance at him. The sun had deepened the colour of his already rich, burnished skin tone. He was wearing a pale grey polo shirt with linen trousers and loafers, and he looked, as always, elegant, understated and very, very expensive.

'Will you miss being here?' she asked idly.

'Tuscany?'

'I mean being here and doing nothing. You've barely worked at all in the past few days.'

Her voice was lazy and light. Gabriel looked at her averted profile, at her face raised to the sun, her eyes concealed behind the sunglasses she was wearing. She was in a loose, swishy skirt, a tight vest and a baseball cap, and she'd never looked sexier.

He frowned. Was that true? He'd done a bit of work

here and there, but in truth, work had taken a back seat to sex. He couldn't remember the last time that had happened, and he wasn't sure he liked it. Or maybe he just wasn't sure *he understood it*.

'How could I?' he drawled. 'When we're supposed to be loved up? How's it going to look if I say good morning and then disappear to put in a full day's work? I would have a nagging wife-to-be to contend with, and what man wants that? Especially when rings aren't even on fingers?'

'You're confusing me with someone else, Gabriel. I'm not the sort of woman who nags.'

'How do you know until you've been married and the guy you thought was going to be there 24-7 spends half his time in an office sitting behind a desk in front of a computer?'

It was dawning on him that, contrary to every ingrained learned behaviour, he had been sleeping with her. Not just *having sex* but *sleeping*. She'd occupied his bed for the past few nights. He'd enjoyed reaching out and feeling her naked body next to his, had enjoyed waking before her and staring at her for a couple of seconds before padding out to make them both a cup of coffee.

She was as casual as he could have possibly hoped for, but even so…thinking about slow steps to a domesticity he was never going to embrace set his teeth on edge and made him remember just what was going on here.

An arrangement with the now added bonus of benefits thrown in. Hearts were never going to be involved. He had no heart to engage. Hurt and love were too entwined for him to trust, and without trust, love could never exist.

And her heart? Not his for the taking, and not one he would ever want to capture.

Hers was a heart destined for a normal guy.

He surfaced from unsettling thoughts to find that she had twisted to look at him.

There was a smudge of chocolate ice cream in the corner of her mouth. He instinctively reached for the paper serviette on the table in front of them and swiped it away. Something swelled inside him at his own unconscious, automatic gesture, and he frowned.

Her pink tongue flicked out, sexy and tantalising, and completed the job.

He was quietly pleased that his instinctive reaction to that glimpse of tongue was to think about sex. There were no disturbing thoughts to deal with when it came to straightforward sex, because that was right in his comfort zone.

He couldn't read the expression in her eyes behind the sunglasses, but he could feel the quiet seriousness in her voice when she spoke.

'I guess,' she said thoughtfully, 'that living in the office, maybe on a camp bed, while the nagging wife waits behind the scenes is your take on marriage.' She smiled wryly. 'Poor woman, if that's your attitude before the whole deal kicks off. Besides, Gabriel, I just don't understand. Why don't you give yourself a chance at taking a risk when it comes to finding a partner?'

'We've talked about this.'

'So we have, but look at it from my point of view. We're here, and we're not even in a proper relationship, yet you've managed to stay away from the computer for...hours on end!'

'Variety is the spice of life,' Gabriel purred silkily. 'It's your fault for being so tempting.'

'Tempting or maybe just different, if variety is the spice of life,' Jennifer quipped, and he remained silent for a few seconds.

'I don't feel hemmed in by you,' Gabriel eventually said. 'You know me, and you know my ground rules, which is why I wanted you to be the one to help me out. Why I chose you. And now that we're sleeping together, I still don't feel hemmed in by you.'

'So it's possible, then…'

'What are you talking about?'

'If you can feel free with me and not in danger of being swamped by someone who wants to cling to you like superglue, then you can feel like that about someone else. And if you throw love and affection into the mix—well, there you have it…'

'There I have what?'

'Don't pretend you don't understand.'

'Life's not so easy, Jen. Maybe for you. Not for me. You lost your father when you were young, but your memories of what a healthy relationship with both your parents looks like are still intact.'

'Yes, but…'

'When I was thirteen, I left home.'

'What?' She turned to him, eyes wide with shock, because this was the first she was hearing anything of this.

Their conversation had been lazy and meandering, touching on the personal without dwelling on it. Now she sat up straight and was paying attention.

How did she not know this about him? For no reason,

she was inexplicably hurt, even though common sense told her that Gabriel was a very private man, that there would probably be lots of things she didn't know about him. Yet being here had fostered a closeness between them that made her think…

Made her think *what*?

She licked her lips and tried to harness her thoughts, which kept evaporating like wisps of smoke when she tried to catch them.

'You *left home*?' She blinked and slowly removed her sunglasses so that now they were staring at one another. She was no longer aware of the busy piazza, of the people bustling all around them…laughing and talking in loud, urgent voices. The vibrant music from the street musician playing close to the busy, colourful market stalls that lined one side of the piazza faded away.

'You left home to do what?' she asked, bewildered. 'A school trip? I'm not following you.'

'I thought it might be a good idea to go see what my father was up to.'

The words hung in the air between them, sucking the oxygen out and leaving a breathless, bated, electrifying silence.

Gabriel looked away from those curious, intelligent, penetrating blue eyes.

He wasn't sure why he had said what he had. It was something he'd never discussed with anyone. That had been a moment in time best forgotten, but now that he had opened up, he didn't regret it.

He stared out, waiting for the inevitable barrage of

questions and wondering whether he would instantly be propelled into resentment.

'Well?' he prodded when nothing was forthcoming.

'Well, what?'

'You sounded shocked by what I said. Were you?'

'I was,' she admitted. 'But I'm not going to pry and be nosy, because I guess you'll probably end up somehow resenting the fact that you shared anything at all. You're private, and you're proud, and those are two big reasons why you'll end up somehow blaming me because you might have confessed to something you'd rather have kept to yourself.'

'Since when did you turn into an amateur psychiatrist?' he asked, but there was fond amusement in his voice, and she smiled.

'Since I teach teenagers who have a tendency to do their utmost to push the envelope just to see how far they can go. Sometimes takes a little forethought to steer them back on the right track.'

'And is that what you're doing? Steering me in the direction you want me to go?'

This time, she did look at him seriously.

'No. I was being honest. Of course I'm curious, but it's up to you if you want to talk about whatever…happened back then and not up to me to try and force you.'

'I don't suppose,' Gabriel said with an indolent shrug, 'that this is any kind of state secret.' Their eyes met, and she raised her eyebrows. 'Okay, I admit it's not something I shout from the rooftops but…when I look back, it was a youthful escapade that was understandable at the time.' He paused, caught the eye of a passing waiter and ordered two glasses of cold, citrusy soda, which was a speciality of the café, and a plate of fresh fruit, along with cornettos con crema for them both.

'My mother made a point of not talking about my dad at all. Their relationship ended, and it was buried underneath silence.' He thought about his past for a few seconds, unfamiliar with the feeling of recounting it verbally. 'I was too young to remember the details, but there were none of the usual arguments or shouting or raised voices.'

'Your mother's not the shouty sort.'

'No,' he agreed, 'but her silence when my father vanished did leave a void, and when I got older, I filled that void with all sorts of childish speculation. By the time I was thirteen, I'd come to the conclusion that my father was out there somewhere, possibly banned from seeing me. But if not, then certainly desperate to make up for lost time with his only son. It was easy to romanticise someone who was never talked about and a situation that was never discussed.'

He sat back as their order was brought to their table. Then they were facing one another as they made inroads into the delicacies in front of them.

'I can't believe I'm eating all this after a gelato,' Jennifer groaned. 'I'm going to get back to England the size of a beached whale.'

Gabriel laughed. If he hadn't wanted to continue with the conversation, her interruption would have provided a natural break, and he knew instinctively that she would have let whatever curiosity she had go. He realised that he wanted to continue.

'I found out where he was living. For an amateur sleuth, it was pretty easy, because my mother had no locked filing cabinets, and the information was there in all the divorce paperwork packed up in neat little folders. If I'd taken the time to actually read through any of it, I might have found out what became apparent when I showed up on his doorstep two days later.'

'What did you find?'

'He'd had a second family whilst he'd been married to my mother. He was open about that. He also had no interest in me whatsoever. He wasn't curious about me, my life or anything I'd done. He couldn't give a damn about the things a parent should give a damn about. He'd walked off, and he'd never looked back. Later, much later, when I was an adult, I discovered the true extent of what he'd done, and it went beyond a second family. He'd fleeced my mother of as much as he possibly could, left the family finances in a precarious position and had done it all without conscience. She'd married him for love. He'd married her for money.'

'I'm sorry, Gabriel. That must have been devastating for you to discover.'

Gabriel shrugged. 'I managed to get the finances back on track as soon as I was old enough to take over the reins, when I found out the true extent of the unholy mess with the divorce settlement and the way he'd trampled over my mother to squeeze as much as he could out of her.'

Jennifer looked at him in silence. His expression was impassive even though he was talking about an event that would have been heartrending.

She hadn't had a clue.

Of course, she would have been too young to have

even grasped the situation all those years ago, but afterward…not a word had been spoken. Her mother and his knew each other well, and yet nothing had filtered down to reach her over the years. He certainly had never breathed a word about that single devastating event in his life.

He'd wiped it from his consciousness and had only revived it now as a way of demonstrating just how immune he was to the concept of love and marriage and what lay at the end of that rainbow.

He might have played truant with work for a few days, and he might have actually allowed her to fall asleep in his bed instead of insisting she return to her bedroom, but had he wanted to impress on her how little both meant in the great scheme of things?

'Did your mum ever talk about how she felt? About your dad? The divorce? What he did?'

'Those would have been conversations best left untouched,' Gabriel said dryly.

'Really? I'm not sure I agree with that, actually.'

'Yes, but you're coming from the perspective of someone who uses cunning psychological tactics to squeeze information from your unsuspecting victims.' He grinned, and Jennifer grinned back at him.

'Don't be mean. You should walk a mile in a teacher's shoes. Sometimes it's the only way.' She looked at him thoughtfully. 'I guess,' she mused pensively, 'that at first your mother wanted to protect you. Then later, maybe too much time had passed. If you never asked any questions, she shied away from volunteering hurtful information. Parents do that. They protect their children. I never knew how ill my father was until he just couldn't hide it any longer.'

'Have you noticed that on a fine, sunny day in one of the most beautiful towns in Italy, we're wasting time having a deep, meaningful conversation about a past that neither of us can change?'

'I suppose that's your way of saying you'd like a change of topic?'

'As I've said so many times before, how well you know me. What do you think of the pastries, by the way? They're quite famous in this part of the world.'

So that insight was now gone, never again to be explored, Jennifer thought, idly lapsing into comfortable conversation and then eventually resuming her lazy people watching in easy silence next to him.

Yet he had fired up a train of thought in her head that was already picking up speed.

Beneath that remote expression, what did he really feel? Did he think about that past that couldn't be changed and feel the pain of that child who was turned away?

Did he think that his mother remained bitter about what had happened?

Was that why he had become so wary of love? Because he'd felt the sting of betrayal on behalf of his mother, whom he dearly loved? With an example set of the worst love could be, had he retreated into the safety of a place sealed off from all emotion, incapable of wanting to find out the very best love could be?

Mostly it was dawning on her just why he remained so aloof in his private life, so determined never to give his heart to anyone.

It wasn't because he could never love anyone. He loved his mother. His heart could hold love. What it couldn't hold was trust. He'd been left without that, and without trust, how could love ever flourish?

He'd made a point of making sure to warn her off getting any ideas into her head that fiction might turn into reality. As much as he could care about anyone outside of his mother, he cared about her. They were friends more than lovers, and he didn't want to see her hurt.

He probably warned all the women he slept with, but he probably didn't care all that much if they chose to ignore his warnings.

Somewhere deep inside her, something felt vaguely broken at the realisation that he really would never commit to anyone, not in any meaningful way.

Had she somehow thought that he'd been exaggerating when he'd said that? Kidding herself? And anyway, did it matter?

She slid her eyes across to him. She could remember him as a teenager, lanky without the muscle mass of the adult, but already with those haughty, chiselled features that made all the girls in the village turn round and stare.

Now he was so much more, and she felt that she could carry on staring at him and thinking about him forever, which made her shift and frown with discomfort.

He was getting too enigmatic for his own good, she thought briskly. She made immediate plans to curb her curiosity. Yet again.

'I suppose we should think about getting back?' she said, standing up and waiting while he took his time to follow suit.

He looked at his watch, something beyond a mere

run-of-the-mill Rolex. She'd once complimented him on it, but all she could remember about it was the fact that you had to put your name on some kind of exclusive waiting list to even be considered as a potential buyer.

'You must be exhausted after sharing so much with me, Gabriel. You probably need a lie-down.'

He stuck on his shades and flashed her a dazzling smile.

'Only if you're in the bed next to me, and I can't guarantee that the only thing we'll be doing is lying down.'

And just like that, they were back in the moment. As they made their way to the vineyards in the four-wheel drive car Gabriel had rented while they were there, the details of what he'd said seemed to fade away.

They chatted about their day, and he impressed her by knowing more about the area than she would have given him credit for.

'You underestimate me,' he said in the sort of tone that implied there was no way he thought that she might actually believe that he wasn't a genius about the details of a small town in Tuscany. 'I know everything.' He slanted her a wicked smile.

'You don't know who's going to be at this party Roberto and Luisa are having for us this evening.'

'No need to know, and why would I care?' He took his hand off the wheel just for a second so that he could slide it over her thigh. 'Probably some local vineyard owners who want to have a little more business chat with me before we leave the day after tomorrow.'

Jennifer shivered. Things would be different in England. They would no longer be in the sun-drenched romantic surroundings of Tuscany, where Gabriel had put work on hold so that they could both forget about the real world for a little while.

Yes, they had decided to continue what had been started. Why not? It made sense to let the inevitable parting of ways happen without pre-empting it, but with a backdrop of reality, she wondered now how long their affair, such as it was, would survive.

When she thought about life post-Gabriel, something inside her hollowed out. Then she couldn't quite see ever again enjoying the easy, innocent friendship they had once had.

In fact, when she thought about life post-Gabriel, she couldn't see anything at all.

'Returning to England is going to be weird,' she now said abruptly, and she felt his dark eyes rest briefly on her averted profile.

'Why?'

'Well, this is a bubble, isn't it? Us? Here? Falling asleep in the same bed? Waking up in the same bed? Work, for you, on the back burner so we're spending all this time together?'

She was edgy and discontented inside. She felt him reach for her hand and idly link his fingers through hers. Her heart constricted when she saw their entwined fingers, his so much darker than hers.

She had a falling, swooping sensation and then a slow trickle of dawning realisations that fell into place.

All this time going on dates with other men, looking for the right guy to come along, the perfect match with whom she would spend the rest of her life. All those high-minded principles and expectations protecting her from a man like Gabriel. *From Gabriel.*

Her mouth went dry and her heart began to beat faster, faster and faster until she could feel a steady throb in her temples.

He was saying something, but there was a roar in her ears, and she was barely taking in what he was saying.

She was too busy realising that the reason love had eluded her was because it had always been there, hiding from her in plain sight.

She loved Gabriel. She *was in love with Gabriel.* He'd been her friend and then, bit by bit, had become so much more than that. He had become the love of her life, and that was the reason every man she'd ever gone out with had somehow felt *not quite right*.

Gabriel had stolen her heart. Now, wrapped up in this charade, she had finally been forced to confront that reality.

What happened next?

'Are you listening to a word I'm saying?'

'Huh?' Jennifer blinked and looked at him, but now she saw him in a different light. This was the man she loved. She could close her eyes and know every part of his dear, beautiful face as well as she knew her own.

And now his body, the body she had traced with her mouth and her hands, tasting and loving it.

'I said,' he repeated slowly but with indulgence and amusement in his voice, 'that in a way, that's a good thing.'

'What are you talking about?'

He laughed. 'Tell me you didn't nod off while I was talking. I think if you did, then my ego might never recover.'

Jennifer heard the familiar light teasing in his voice,

and it hit her hard just how much more she wanted from him than that.

'You have an ego, Gabriel? Shocking.' She fell in with the familiar relationship they'd always had, even now when everything had changed, but her heart continued to beat like a sledgehammer inside her as she adjusted to a realisation she wished she'd never had. 'When I always thought you were such a modest guy.'

'Reality,' he explained. 'Reality is going back to my work schedule and you back to yours. It's going to put a toll on this, and it'll be natural when things begin unravelling until it fizzles out and we're left where we started.'

'It can never really be where it started, though, can it?'

'Is this a general statement or something that's leading up to an in-depth discussion of something that's not worth discussing?'

'What do you mean, *something that's not worth discussing*?'

'I suppose,' he said slowly but honestly, 'we're committed to going with the flow, and I won't lie when I say that I like where we are at the moment. What's the point in speculating about what happens when all this is over? And trying to predict how we'll feel or what we'll feel? When we get back, I intend to try and spend more time with my mother. I'll be seeing you more often than I normally would. We can go house-hunting together and live in the moment.'

'What?' For a second her mind went completely blank. Then she got excited about searching for a house to share with this glorious man. What would *a life to share* look like?

For a fleeting second, reality and fantasy merged, and she was swept away on a tide of pure joy.

'What on earth are you talking about, Gabriel? What house?'

'Don't panic,' he said wryly. 'I haven't suddenly decided to become domesticated. Don't forget I'm paying you for what you're doing here.'

Jennifer blinked at him and looked away.

'Actually, I *had* forgotten.'

'Well, it's time to start remembering. I would have given you a lot more, but you'll certainly have enough to put down a very healthy deposit on the house of your dreams—which, incidentally, is where, exactly?'

'Gabriel, it doesn't feel right to pay me now that we're…we're…'

'Why not?' He frowned and didn't bother to pretend to misunderstand.

Jennifer knew in that moment that for him, nothing had changed. Sex was sex. It didn't leach into other areas of his life, and it certainly wasn't suddenly tied up in tormenting realisations about love and desires and yearnings for more than was on the table.

'Feels weird,' she said limply.

'Won't feel weird when we're looking at houses.'

'Won't you be bored doing that?' Jennifer asked, giving up on trying to get her garbled message across. 'Have you ever actually been house-hunting before?'

'No, now that you mention it.' He glanced across at her. 'When I want a house somewhere, I instruct my executive assistant to do all the necessary groundwork. I just give my approval to one when I'm presented with the shortlist, and after that, the interior designers take over.'

Jennifer burst out laughing. 'Honestly, you really don't live in the real world.'

'It's very real to me,' he protested, but he was grinning. 'A lot of legwork went into checking over the final tally for my place in London, although in truth, when it involves buying a place abroad, I leave the entire production to someone on the ground in whatever country I'm buying it in.'

'Well, won't it be a treat to traipse round potential houses with you and talk about wallpaper stripping and reconfiguring a kitchen. Think you'll be able to handle it?'

'Depends on the reward afterward.'

'What sort of reward are you talking about?'

'I could show you if I find a suitably quiet spot somewhere off the beaten track on the way back. What are your thoughts on making love in an open field with nothing but the sky above us and olive groves all around?'

Bloody wonderful. 'Very bad idea because we're running late as it is, considering we have to be back for this party Roberto and Luisa are having for us.'

'Shame. Maybe another time.'

'Is sex really all you think about, Gabriel?'

'No, work always tops the list. Except for now.'

Jennifer didn't say anything, but beneath the torment of realising that she'd fallen in love with the most inaccessible man on the planet, small shoots of hope began to stir.

Of course, she knew the danger of hope, but still…

Was it significant that here with her, he had forgotten about work? Was it significant that here with her, he had spent the nights in the same bed?

And most important of all, was it significant that before they'd even touched, they'd been friends? That their friendship had been deep and meaningful?

They would continue seeing one another…until they didn't. He would be waiting and expecting that being back in reality would eventually reassert all the boundary lines between them. He might think that work, once again, would top the list when it came to his priorities, but if she were to be patient, might he find that she was less dispensable than he imagined?

Might being lovers have added so much to their relationship that he wouldn't be able to distance himself from her the way he assumed?

She told herself to get a grip on her imagination, to stop seeing a future that wasn't there. She told herself that he was a man who would never trust enough to be open to love, who was too conditioned by his past… But it was difficult to listen to those reasonable voices when she badly wanted to believe that the love she had for him would be returned.

They could see from all the lights on at the main house that preparations were in full swing for the guests who had been invited for dinner.

'I blame you if we're late,' he murmured, hopping out of the car and swinging round to open her door for her.

She stepped out, but as she opened her mouth to laughingly protest, he covered it with his. The meshing of their tongues made him harden in instant response. They were invisible here from prying eyes, and he blindly reached down to push his hand under her skirt and then down into her knickers. He found the tiny nub of her clitoris, already stiffened and pulsing. He teased and rubbed it until she was breathing and panting and then…shuddering as an orgasm ripped through her, leaving her limp and gasping against him.

'Gabriel!'

'I know, my darling. It felt good for me, too…'

Jennifer thought, *For the first time, he called me his darling...*

Then the moment was lost as he teasingly told her to stop distracting him, to save the distractions for later, when they were back in bed and he could take her the way he knew she liked being taken…

'And we won't be long at whatever party they're throwing,' he promised when, an hour later, they were dressed and walking towards the main house.

He had his arm slung over her shoulder. Through the thin, shimmering jade-green dress she had flung on for the party, she could feel the hard muscularity of his body. Her mind was already racing ahead to just what they'd be getting up to when they were back in their cottage as they knocked on the front door of the main house. It was pulled open before she could knock twice. Luisa was right there, with Roberto bouncing happily behind her.

'You are here!' Luisa was urging them in towards the fragrant smells of food cooking and the sound of voices and laughter, although there weren't as many people there as either of them had expected. There had only been a few cars in the courtyard. 'Come, come! There is someone so eager to meet you!'

'And we can't wait to meet your children,' Gabriel was saying politely.

They laughed, and then Luisa said with a lot of happy gesturing, '*Non stai incontrando I miei figli! Stai in-*

contrando don Alfonso, il prete del paese! E qui per benedirvi entrambi!'

Jennifer smiled glassily and then turned to Gabriel.

'Translation, please, Gabriel?'

'We're not meeting their kids, Jen.' He paused and raked his fingers through his hair. 'We're meeting the local priest, who's come to bless us…'

CHAPTER NINE

BLESS THEM? HOW? Why? Had she even heard correctly?

In a daze, Jennifer found herself herded affectionately into the sitting room, where things were in full swing.

It had been decorated for the occasion with beautiful scented candles positioned on the shelves. There were no more than a dozen people. Francesca was chatting in a group of elderly people who were sitting on sofas by the huge stone fireplace. Two other couples, roughly the same age, in their late sixties, were laughing and talking, glasses of red wine in their hands. Luisa was in her element, although as soon as they walked in, she turned to them, her face wreathed in a smile.

There wasn't the formality of anyone serving hors d'oeuvres. Instead, there were small plates of bruschetta on the polished wooden sideboard, as well as olives and cheeses and various types of bread.

'Come, come, children! But don't fill up on the snacks. There will be a lot of food served shortly.'

Francesca was hurrying over to them, and everyone else took that as their cue to gather around. There was no getting away from the fact that she and Gabriel were the reluctant centre of attention.

Father Giovanni was introduced with pride, followed by everyone else.

'I'm never going to remember all the names.' Jennifer laughed. 'I should because I teach, but honestly, as soon as I leave the classroom, my head for names disappears.'

'She's a wonderful teacher,' Francesca said proudly. 'My son, who's always worked all the hours under the sun, couldn't hope for a better catch. This darling girl doesn't put up with unruly pupils, and she would never put up with an unruly husband!'

Dear Lord, Jennifer thought faintly, *now we're practically married.*

'No one could ever tell Gabriel what to do,' she said, and she felt him move towards her and give her an affectionate squeeze.

'Since when has that ever stopped you?' he murmured to approving nods. 'This woman has been telling me off since she was ten.'

'That's not true, Gabriel!' Their eyes met, and she felt her heart flutter. Had she? She'd certainly never held back when it came to voicing her opinions.

'You were the only person to tell me to stop showing off when I bought my first car.'

'It was a stupid car.' *And a dangerous one*... She could remember the conversation as if it had happened yesterday, and she could also remember the horror she had felt at the thought of losing him to a car accident. What idiot, she had told him acerbically, decided to buy a high-end fast car at the age of eighteen *because he could*?

'I think you just proved my point.'

Their eyes tangled and her tummy flipped over this time, and she had to keep staring until she was in danger of running out of breath. At which point she rolled her eyes and looked away, shaken by just how powerful the connection was.

'Do you hear that, Father Giovanni?' Luisa turned to the elderly priest and drew him close to them. 'Francesca tells me that her son is a changed man. Hasn't buried himself in work for the first time since he and Jennifer got here.'

'I've never known him to do that before,' Francesca agreed. 'And I've lectured him a million times on the importance of not working too hard. Jennifer has been able to reach parts of my son I never could.'

'Which is a good sign.' Father Giovanni nodded approvingly. He directed them towards a table at the side which was laden with tasty cold appetizers.

Just when Jennifer thought that an audience might be appreciated, everyone seemed to have evaporated into the background by mutual consent, leaving the three of them to fill their plates and then retire to a clutch of chairs towards the back of the sprawling sitting room.

'I do not usually do this sort of thing…' Father Giovanni ate and spoke between mouthfuls of garlic prawn and rustic bread, dabbing his chin after every mouthful.

He was as round as his host and with the same kind, weather-beaten, tanned face. A priest his flock would adore.

'And you shouldn't feel you have to…er…do anything,' Jennifer interrupted, sliding her eyes sideways to where Gabriel was sitting in easy silence, sipping some red wine, his long legs stretched to the side. 'Luisa and Roberto are so thoughtful, but they've already done enough for us without…er…'

Father Giovanni waved aside the stuttering interruption. 'It is my pleasure, and—' he nodded to Gabriel '—I believe your charming mother was very keen on the idea of you both being blessed. It is nothing formal, my children, but I hope it remains with you as you move through your married life.'

'We haven't set a date or anything yet,' Jennifer managed. 'So…'

'You have known each other a long time, I understand?'

Gabriel finally decided to speak. 'Like I said, she's been a thorn in my side since she was a child.'

'From friendship often comes the strongest glue to bind two souls together.'

Jennifer felt her heart jump because this mirrored just what she had dared to think herself.

'Do you really believe that?' she asked, raising her eyebrows whilst hanging on to his every word.

'I sincerely do,' the priest said, half turning to address her. He carefully balanced his plate on his knees and linked his fingers together on his stomach. 'We little realise how important it is that we know the small things about the people we end up spending our lives with. Too often, those details get lost in the fluff of being in love. Then, when they do get recognised, they become the obstacles that lie in the path to true happiness.'

'The divorce rate,' Gabriel murmured from alongside her, 'certainly proves that most people do a lot of getting lost in the fluff.'

'But,' Jennifer risked, head tilted to one side, 'some manage to make their way out.'

'Well spoken, my child. I do not want to monopolise

the pair of you this evening, so I will just tell you to beware the pitfalls that lie ahead.'

'Do you have sufficient time to list them all, Father?' Gabriel grinned. 'We leave the country pretty soon…'

'There are only a few to watch out for, young man.' Father Giovanni wagged his finger with a smile before sipping some of his wine. 'Arguments over money…'

'Ring any bells, Jen?'

Jennifer glared at him, remembering how she had initially knocked him back for daring to offer her money to pretend to be in a relationship with him.

'He has way too much money,' she said to the priest. 'No one needs as many cars as Gabriel has, so if we argue, it's only because I like to point out the obvious to him.'

'She's been arguing with me about money for a long time, so we're clearly not off to a good start when it comes to making it to the finishing line.'

Father Giovanni was smiling indulgently at them.

'So, we have the money arguments…' The priest ticked that one off on a finger. 'And of course we have the complacency trap, so I counsel you to always make one another feel special.'

Gabriel reached out and linked his fingers through hers. When he squeezed them, she knew just what was going through his mind. They had been doing a great job of making one another feel special recently.

'Let us not forget the curse of the in-laws!' Father Giovanni ended with a wink.

Jennifer looked at Gabriel just as he stole a sidelong glance at her. Her breath caught in her throat before he broke eye contact to briefly lower his gaze.

'That's one area where there's nothing at all to worry about,' he said gruffly. 'Jen's almost as close to my mother as I am, and her mother thinks I'm the best thing since sliced bread.'

'You know something I don't. I've never actually heard those words cross her lips!' But she was smiling, because her mother was indeed very fond of Gabriel. 'He makes things up as he goes along. Honestly—' she was still linking fingers with Gabriel when she looked at Father Giovanni '—he has an ego the size of a cruise liner.' She heard Gabriel chuckle and was flooded with warmth and tenderness and love.

All taboo. All there. Love…tenderness…desire…and a crazy craving for him never to leave her side.

'I bless you, my children, and it goes without saying that my wish is for your love to grow stronger by the day and for you to be blessed with the gift of many children.'

What had Gabriel made of that?

She hadn't expected the priest to have touched her so deeply. Inside her, something had shifted. She muddled her way through the remainder of the evening and enjoyed herself, but she couldn't remember any of what she had said to any of the lovely people there when, finally, they were saying good-night to Francesca, with Gabriel escorting his mother up the stairs to her bedroom.

'Well,' Jennifer said as she and Gabriel made their way back to their cottage. 'On a scale of one to ten…?'

'I've had more comfortable experiences.'

He stepped back to let her precede him and then quietly closed the door behind them.

A blessing?

What had he expected when Luisa had told him that that would be on the menu, along with home-cooked pasta and the finest of red wines?

Had he honestly expected a *comfortable experience*?

Truth was, he hadn't really given it a huge amount of thought. It would be something to be navigated with politeness and almost zero personal participation, over in the blink of an eye and duly put on the back burner.

But something had got to him. Father Giovanni had moved him, and he wasn't sure he'd liked that. It had taken him by surprise, which was something else he'd never had much time for.

'I never saw myself as a father of many children,' he mused with a grin. 'How many is *many*, I wonder. Football team? Bigger? Maybe I should have delved deeper into that particular aspect of the blessing.'

'I was actually being serious.'

'Why, Jen? It was something unavoidable. Why dwell on it?' But he remembered the uncomfortable way it had made him feel, as though he was gently being channelled into thoughts he didn't want. The memory reinforced his need to dismiss the blessing neither of them had asked for and all uncomfortable thoughts along with it. 'It wasn't what I expected,' he confessed eventually.

'What were you expecting?'

'Something vague and well-meaning in between the bruschetta and the main course, I suppose.'

He went to the fridge, got himself a bottle of water and drank it in one go. Then he looked at her.

She'd shone all evening. She'd looked beautiful in her slinky jade-green dress, with her long, dark hair tumbling down her back and her voluptuous curves radiating the sort of sexiness no amount of money could buy. She had smiled and chatted with everyone. She'd fitted in because she had the special knack of putting people at ease.

No wonder his mother was so thrilled at the thought of her becoming Mrs Gabriel Garcia, if she chose to take his name—and who knew, because the woman had a mind of her own. No wonder his mother was even now probably musing whether her first grandchild would be a girl or a boy and debating where she should buy her mother-of-the-groom outfit.

Looking at Jennifer now, he felt the same disturbing edginess he had felt during the course of the evening, and never more so than when the priest had blessed them, when he'd solemnly told them about the sanctity of marriage and the importance of trying to make it work in a world that was filled with doubt and uncertainties.

'Sex?' he suggested as if he might be offering her a drink.

'Well,' she laughed, 'that's a novel approach to foreplay.'

'There are times when foreplay is overrated.'

'And now is one of them?'

'It's the dress. It's been doing all sorts of things to my libido this evening.'

'Tell me more.'

'Better if I show you what I mean…'

He stepped towards her with intent, losing himself in the physical, yet knowing that once it was over, once they were both sated, he would have to face that disturbing edginess and do something to put a full stop to it.

There was no point thinking that he was going to

take his time. That would have to come another day, but right now…

He'd never wanted anyone as much as he wanted her. He wanted to lose himself in her, to drown out the unsettling feelings swirling inside him that he couldn't seem to pin down and reason away.

They stumbled towards the bedroom, shedding clothes along the way. Her fingers scrabbled to unbutton his trousers. By the time they were in the bedroom, he had pushed down her dress, and she had somehow managed to wriggle out of it and kick it somewhere. Anywhere.

What remained of their clothing was ripped off at speed before they hit the mattress, and then…

He couldn't wait. He was going crazy just touching her and feeling the soft, heavy weight of her breasts, the stiffness of her nipples. Her soft cries urged him on, and he thrust into her, long and deep and hard, again and again, as she wrapped her long legs around him. Was he expunging something from within himself? It felt like it, but he didn't know what.

He knew that she came with him. He could feel the stiffening of her body and hear the urgency of her guttural moans.

He half opened his eyes to look at her. He wanted to see the mounting colour in her face and the flaring of her nostrils and the fluttering of her eyes as she soared away on an orgasm that peaked just as he arched up and came with a long, violent shudder.

Lying against him, Jennifer had never felt closer. To him or to anyone. Never.

This was what love felt like, and she was surprised

that she had only now slotted the pieces of this jigsaw together and understood her feelings for what they were.

The way they had made love…

There had been a hot, frantic urgency there, something strong and powerful that had spoken of feelings in him that matched hers. Or was she imagining that?

She wriggled against him and stroked his spine with her finger, dragging her blunt nail along it. He shivered and half laughed against her neck.

'So…' she said softly, and she pulled back to look at him. It was dark in the room, but not so dark that she couldn't make out the drowsy, unfocused look in his eyes, the look of a man who had just had his every need met.

'So?'

'We were talking about what Father Giovanni said to us…'

'Were we?'

'Yes. Before you decided that we had to have sex without delay. Gabriel, how did you feel when he blessed our union?'

'Haven't we covered that?' he groaned. 'About the same time as I was musing on how big this mythical family of mine was going to be and whether I'd need a house extension?' He flung himself back and shielded his eyes with his arm for a couple of seconds. Then he flipped onto his side and looked at her. 'You were impressive tonight,' he murmured.

Jennifer smiled, touched by the husky sincerity in his voice, as though he hadn't been able to resist the spontaneous compliment.

'Keep talking…'

'Beautiful and engaging and impressive. You have a genuine interest in other people and what they have to say, and don't tell me that it's because you teach and you're paid to listen to those brats of yours waffle on about nonsense all day long.'

'You realise that you were once a brat just like them?'

'My teachers all loved me.'

'That's your ego talking again, and I think you're trying to change the subject. We were chatting about Father Giovanni and what he said. I wanted to know how you felt about that.'

'Okay. I think I felt awkward,' he said, idly toying with her hair.

'Why?'

'Because that's not what we're about.'

'Yes, I know.' She hesitated. Then, for a few seconds, she felt as though she was staring down into a deep, deep abyss.

She loved him. She always had. The love had grown from the ground up, from adoring hero worship when she'd been a kid to deep friendship to a crush she hadn't even really known she'd harboured all the way through to this…this wonderful thing that filled her up now, every bit of her.

Should she wait to see whether he could ever feel the same? Would waiting in hopeful silence bring her any closer to her dream, or would he remain oblivious to any feelings he might have for her, any feelings that might go beyond simple friendship?

What the priest had said about friendship and love echoed in her ears now. Hadn't that been the very thing she'd been thinking?

How could she keep this to herself? She would never be able to go on another date again if she didn't tell him how she felt now, because she would be too busy spending her life waiting for him…thinking about her love… just *loving him.*

The best that could happen was that he would see what she saw, would recognise the feelings they had for one another as something bigger than either of them could ever have expected.

And if he didn't?

If he turned away from her…?

It was a sobering thought, but at least rejection would bring clarity and enable her to move on with her life. She'd wasted so much time and energy dating guys only to methodically pick them apart, not knowing that none of them had ever stood a chance next to the friend she had fallen in love with.

Whatever happened, saying how she felt would open doors for her to a different way forward. All at once she knew that the time for that had come.

'Penny for them.'

'Sorry?' Jennifer blinked and refocused.

'You're a million miles away.' He smiled. 'I don't like that. I much prefer a Jennifer who's in the here and now with me. What's going through that pretty little head of yours?'

'Pretty little head of mine?' Momentarily distracted, she rolled her eyes and heaved an exaggerated sigh. 'You know you can't say stuff like that, don't you?'

'But you are very pretty.'

'You're teasing me.'

'Of course I am. I'm a twenty-first-century man, which means I'm a feminist.'

She decided that they could both get lost in this line of good-natured banter because it was well-trodden ground, but right now, there were more important things to talk about. If she didn't talk about them now, then who knew when she would next drum up the courage?

'What Father Giovanni said made me think, Gabriel.' She felt him still and breathed in deeply. 'Before, we were just having a bit of fun, but when he talked about marriage and about what it entailed, it actually made me realise that…that…'

'Don't, Jennifer.'

'You don't even know what I'm going to say.'

'I can tell from the expression on your face that I'm probably not going to…know what to do with whatever you think you may want to say. I don't like situations where I don't know what to do.'

'That makes the two of us, Gabriel, but…' She closed her eyes tightly, then opened them and looked at him without blinking. 'I love you. Don't interrupt. Just let me talk. I love you. Not just like a friend, but more than that. I'm in love with you. I don't think I realised it before, but when Father Giovanni began talking to us, when he blessed us as though we were really and truly a couple, something inside me realised that, to me, we were. A couple.' She raised one finger and gently placed it over his beautiful mouth even though he hadn't started to say anything. 'In my heart, we've always been a couple. In my heart, you've always been the man for me. I just never realised it. But now…'

She looked at him. His face was inscrutable.

'We could give this a chance,' she told him in a rush. 'I mean a proper chance. I know you're afraid of...getting your heart broken, but we go back a long way, Gabriel, and whether you dare admit it or not, we're very much suited to one another.'

In that moment, looking into her honest, beautiful, intelligent blue eyes, Gabriel at last understood the source of that edginess he'd been feeling recently, an edginess that had been there from the first moment he'd touched her. Or maybe even before. Certainly it had been there when Father Giovanni had chatted to them about marriage and the importance of overcoming the pitfalls.

It was the sickening discomfort that sprang from fear. Gabriel hadn't recognised its provenance because fear was an emotion that largely didn't generally register on his radar.

He'd felt fear, the fear of temptation. He'd thought about her, about her being by his side and never leaving it. He'd been terrified because the thought had stirred something deep inside him, something that resembled hope.

Hope for what? Love? Hope that the stupid fantasies accompanying love might be true for him? That the stories people told about love being the thing money could never buy might actually work? Hope in what the priest had said, with all that sincerity and earnest conviction?

Not for him, he thought fiercely as he continued to drown in her questioning, earnest blue eyes. Never for him.

Love meant trust—and trust, when it was broken,

resulted in the sort of pain he'd felt once and never intended to feel again.

And then there was her heart, pure and open. When that got broken, it would never be pieced together again. She would be like him, locked away in an ivory tower with walls too high for anyone to penetrate.

He had no intention of being the man who ended up breaking her heart.

Inside himself, though, something was splintering, because he knew he had to turn away from her. He squeezed his eyes tightly shut for a couple of seconds, putting a stop to the anguish that threatened to tear him apart.

She'd said she loved him, but she would recover in due course and find someone she deserved.

She would thank him when the hurt had passed and her pride had been put back together again. If he were to encourage the illusion that they could actually make things work between them…when it failed, what they had would never recover.

The mere thought that he had flirted with the notion of it at all made his jaw clench, because it was a weakness he had never anticipated having to deal with.

'Now,' he heard her say, 'it's my turn to ask what's going through your head.'

'You think you love me, Jen,' he rasped unsteadily, 'but you don't. We're here…and the strangeness, the scenery…and then that blessing…it's all made you think that there's more to this than what there actually is.' He thought about his own weakness, the way he'd slipped so easily into the habit of sharing a bed with her, putting her ahead of work—flirting with the impossible.

Steel solidified inside him as he automatically recoiled at his own susceptibility. 'As for me? I've told you that I'm not built for what you're looking for, and it was naive of you to ever think that somehow anything would have changed on that front. Jen, you know more about me than anyone else. You should understand that the lessons I've learnt from my parents' divorce, from the cynicism of my father using my mother for money, from the way I was firmly turned away when I was idiotic enough to think there might be feelings for me, his own child, there…well, all of that is the foundation that has made me who I am.'

Jennifer sucked in a shaky breath.

Her nakedness made her feel vulnerable and humiliated and foolish. Hope, which had felt so solid such a short time ago, had evaporated as quickly as dew on a hot summer's morning.

She began pulling away and then froze when he stayed her with fierce desperation.

'I get the message,' she mumbled.

'I've hurt you.'

'You've been honest, and I can only be thankful for that. I… I don't know what got into me.'

'You were overwhelmed by everything out here. The icing on the cake was Father Giovanni and his well-intentioned sermon on love and marriage.'

Jennifer knew that he was throwing her a lifeline. She could pretend that yes, it had all been an inconvenient rush of blood to the head. Of course she didn't love him! Of course she hadn't given her heart to him! She'd just found herself swept away in the moment, probably because of that blessing, which was something neither of them had counted on.

After all, hadn't things been ticking along quite nicely before Father Giovanni had appeared on the scene?

'Maybe,' she said.

'There's no *maybe* about it.'

'You're right,' she said quietly. 'There's no *maybe* about it. I love you, Gabriel, and there's no point pretending that I don't, that this is just some sort of holiday romance that'll go away once reality kicks in.'

'You said…'

'I know *what I said*.' She flung her hands up in frustration and impatience. 'I know I told you that you were the last man I would ever be interested in settling down with. I *know* your idea of a relationship is something that lasts ten seconds before you get bored and start looking at your watch because you know it's time to move on.'

'That's hardly fair.'

'That's *one hundred percent fair*!' She leapt from the bed, dragging the sheet off to sketchily cover herself, suddenly livid with him and with herself. She didn't care that she was still flushed from making love. She stood by the side of the bed, clumsily clutching the sheet, her body leaning belligerently towards him, her long, dark hair falling around her shoulders in an unruly tangle. Her blue eyes were narrowed with anger.

'Don't do that,' Gabriel muttered in a harsh, shaky growl.

'Do *what*? Tell you how I feel? Speak my mind? I'm not a puppet you can control! I don't have to say what you want to hear just because you don't enjoy feeling uncomfortable!'

'I know you're not a puppet, Jen!' Gabriel bellowed back with equally frustrated ferocity.

He rolled out of the bed to stand in front of her, his body language as combatant as hers but with no sheet covering his nakedness.

'Since when,' he imparted with an impatient slash of his hand, 'have you ever tiptoed around me?'

'Never! And that's why I'm not tiptoeing now, either! You're welcome to find yourself some silly little woman who doesn't stand up to you and is willing to do as they're told!'

'It's not about that,' Gabriel muttered in a driven undertone.

'You're just scared to get involved with anyone. You're scared that you might end up getting hurt, but what's life about if you never take chances?'

'This is an impossible conversation!'

But he didn't turn away. His eyes drifted down from the hectic flush of her cheeks, the angry flare in her eyes, to all those places the sheet was barely covering.

'Don't you *dare*!' she snapped.

'Dare what?' He raked his fingers through his hair and glared at her.

'Look at me!'

'You mean the way you're looking at me?'

Jennifer felt her breath hitch in her throat. He was just so beautiful, so unashamedly masculine and so outrageously turned on. His proud erection felt like a personal challenge, throwing her into turmoil and just daring her to touch.

Had she been looking at him?

Yes. It was a shameful admission. How could she resist? She breathed quickly, nostrils flaring as she tried to peel her eyes away from him and yank her disobedient thoughts back under control.

'You stand there telling me all this,' he said shakily, 'and what I want to do is…'

Jennifer opened her mouth to tell him in *no uncertain terms* that the last thing she wanted was for him to touch her. Then he touched her, and every bone in her body melted.

'I'm not interested,' she moaned, reaching to shamelessly wind her arms around his neck and feeling the sheet slither to the ground to pool at her feet. The hard push of his length against her was irresistible. She reached down to grip it in her hands, to caress it the way she knew he loved, her rhythm firm and slow and in time with the throb of his response.

'Jennifer…'

'One last time,' she whispered. 'And then…'

'And then what?'

'We part company. The next time you see me, the person who loved you will be gone forever.'

CHAPTER TEN

JENNIFER PEERED INTO the dim, shadowy bowels of the pub, wondering whether she would recognise her date and fighting off a sickening feeling of déjà vu.

She'd been here before.

Online date. Disappointing guy. Hurried glances at her watch. Philosophical reasoning that she'd have better luck next time. She was getting right back on the horse in an attempt at distraction because it seemed the best idea. The alternative was moping and crying and just… *thinking way too much for her own good.*

It had been three months since she had said goodbye to Gabriel. Three months! A lot had happened during those three months, and yet in a weird way, it felt as though time hadn't moved on at all. She was stuck in the same groove, with a broken heart, saying her last goodbye to the only man she'd ever loved, lost and drifting on tides that were taking her nowhere.

She refocused.

The pub was a traditional London pub. It was a Grade-II-listed building with a lot of dark oak fittings and wood panelling and long wooden tables with benches. At six thirty in the evening, the place was heaving. You could barely hear yourself think. Everyone was escaping the icy clutch of the oncoming winter outside. There were people at the bar, people in the bright restaurant area she could see just beyond the lounge area and a few families in the cosy snug adjoining the bar.

And a lone guy with a beard sitting at a table in the corner, nursing a pint.

She pinned a smile on her face and wound her way between the tables to join him.

'Colin?'

'That's me, babe! Get you a drink?'

He was rising to his feet, and Jennifer already knew that disappointment lay ahead.

He was shorter than she'd expected. Maybe she should have checked his profile a little more thoroughly. She was tall. Height mattered, whether she wanted to admit it or not. He was also plumper than she'd thought, which just made her think of Gabriel with his fabulous body and lazy, muscular sexuality. She felt the familiar urge to start crying.

'I'll have a white wine.'

He looked a little taken aback.

'Or a diet cola.'

'Great!' He nodded. 'I'll grab us some crisps. Salt and vinegar do for you?'

'Not for me,' Jennifer said politely. 'I'm actually dieting at the moment.'

That elicited an assessing stare from him, and he nodded again, which made her think he agreed that yes, a diet was a good idea. Which in turn made her hackles rise, but she kept smiling through bared teeth.

She wasn't sure whether she could be bothered with

the inevitable chit-chat about nothing in particular before one of them made some kind of lame excuse to leave.

She would ask him about himself and show some polite interest, but she would be thinking about how much her life had changed since she'd returned from Italy.

No more living at home with her mother. No more Suffolk. No more teaching at the local school in a routine she had perfected over the years.

Instead, she had seen the money Gabriel had insisted on paying her land in her account when she'd returned to England, and the tantalising thought of *escape* had beckoned. In fact, he had deposited a hell of a lot more money into her account than they had agreed. He'd obviously felt guilty about knocking her back.

She hadn't complained.

Why should she?

If he felt guilty because he'd walked away when she'd opened up her heart to him, then that was just fine with her. She wasn't going to be a martyr and wring her hands while telling him that no, she couldn't possibly accept more than they had agreed.

She'd gone to London, registered with two estate agents and found somewhere to buy within the week.

She hadn't been fussy.

Small house…two bedrooms so that she could rent one out to her friend Alicia, who had arranged interviews at the school where she now worked. She had pulled strings and put in a load of good words and managed to get her a maternity cover job that would tide her over until she could find something permanent. A sweet, small house in a safe area in a part of southwest London that she knew, because she had a couple of friends in the area, girls she'd been on her teaching course with years before and with whom she kept in touch.

As a cash buyer in a buyer's market, she'd had her pick of places, and had chosen a little terraced house in Sheen with vacant possession. She had been able to move in within seven weeks.

And she'd said goodbye, just like that, to everything she'd ever known.

'So, Colin,' she said as he settled into the chair opposite her, with another pint for himself and her diet cola, 'your profile says that you work in IT. It sounds fascinating...'

Gabriel looked at the address that his mother had texted to him. She'd even added *London... England* after the postcode for good measure.

'You're getting in touch with Jennifer?' she had asked casually, but he had detected the hope in her voice and had been determined not to encourage it. Who knew what would happen when he contacted her? If he chose to contact her. No, why kid himself, he was definitely going to get in touch with her. He had to. He'd been going crazy.

Three months was a long time.

Especially when he thought about how things had ended between them. A declaration of love from her and a swift rebuttal from him. Hell, he had even tried to persuade her that she was making a mistake in thinking that she had feelings for him, as though somehow a change of scenery and a little Mediterranean heat had gone to her head and made her hallucinate.

He'd tried every trick in the book to avoid the response he'd known she'd wanted to hear.

Love?

Love was a weakness that led to pain. He had slammed the door shut on any response to her declaration of love but the one that was negative.

They had made love for the last time, and he had felt an urge to cry, but of course he hadn't. Instead, he had followed her cue, had resumed some level of superficial amicable communication so that they could mug along for the remainder of their time with his mother until they returned to England.

At which point he had feigned important meetings in Hong Kong and had promptly disappeared for a fortnight.

'Can't be helped,' he had told his mother in a phone call. 'I had a lot of time off in Italy, and it's catching up with me. No such thing as a free lunch, or whatever that saying is…'

He'd tried to contact Jennifer, but his texts had gone unanswered, and his calls had gone to voicemail.

And he was going crazy.

With memories…with sorrow…with remorse.

Every day, another piece of the puzzle had slotted into place, and the friendship that had seemed so straightforward morphed seamlessly into a love that had grown like a weed until it had invaded every corner of his life without him noticing its advance.

He had turned away from the only woman he had ever loved. Living with that growing realisation had made him feel sick.

It took very little time for him to head out of his office, summon his driver and take the fastest route to the address his mother had texted him.

Jennifer was in a daze.

Two pints for him had somehow turned into three, she was on her second diet cola, and the packet of crisps had evolved into a plate of fries drowning in ketchup.

'I'm ravenous,' Colin had said when he'd ordered the fries. 'Don't mind, do you? With your diet and everything? I mean, feel free to have some. Of course, I can get you something…' He'd frowned and looked a little vague. 'A salad? I'm not a fan of those, but I guess that's the sort of stuff you're eating to lose weight?'

'I'm fine,' she said.

The moment to leave seemed to have been missed, and now she felt as though she would simply have to ride the date out, wait until he'd run out of steam talking about himself and then make her escape.

She'd always been far too well-mannered when it came to ditching men after ten minutes on the first date.

She was listening to him go on at length about various routes he had taken to various jobs in various counties to fix various computer issues when she saw him glance over her shoulder.

'Think someone's looking for you, babe.'

'No one knows I'm here.'

'He's heading straight in this direction.' He picked something from between his teeth and helped himself to another chip.

Jennifer turned around and felt this really was déjà vu. For a few devastating seconds, her heart actually seemed to stop beating, and her brain went into tumultuous meltdown.

Gabriel.

The last person she expected to see and yet the only one she wanted to. She wondered whether she was hallucinating, whether she had managed to conjure up the guy standing in front of her from her feverish imagination, a grim optical illusion there to persecute her even more than she already had been.

He was in charcoal-grey work trousers and a white shirt and a jacket. As he walked towards them, he began removing his tan trench coat.

People surreptitiously swivelled to stare as he made his way through the crowded pub, his dark eyes lasered to her face.

Jennifer began to stand as he closed in on them.

'Gabriel…' she breathed shakily when he was within touching distance of her. 'What are you doing here?' She bunched her hands into fists and stuck them behind her back. Her temples were throbbing, and the crowd around them had faded away, leaving just the two of them staring at one another.

Once they were friends. Now she looked at him with simmering hostility as the hurt of rejection swamped her.

'I've come to see you.'

'Well, I don't want to see *you*.'

'Jen, please…'

'I don't want to have a scene here with you, Gabriel, so you should just go away and leave me alone.'

'You're angry with me, and I can't blame you.'

Jennifer felt tears begin to push through, and she blinked them away. 'I'm not angry with you, Gabriel,' she said thickly. 'I'm angry with myself. Look…this isn't a good time.'

'I really want to talk to you. What happened between us…it's…it's been tearing me apart.'

Jennifer heard the driven sincerity in his voice, but she refused to be swayed by it. If he had come to talk about the friendship they had lost, then what could she say? Right now, friendship wasn't what she wanted from him. Maybe one day, when the rawness of rejection had faded and she'd regained some kind of perspective. Maybe then they could have a conversation about piecing their friendship back together.

Yet as their eyes held, she could see the lines of exhaustion on his face, and the plea in them made her heart treacherously constrict.

She turned away abruptly and felt his hand on her arm, gentle but firm. Then she felt him move closer, felt his warm breath on her neck.

'Tell your date that you're leaving.'

'I'll do no such thing!' She awkwardly stumbled around to face him and wished she hadn't. He was so close, and his proximity made her dizzy as memories and hurt and pain crashed through into the present.

'Hey, mate!'

Both of them looked at Colin, who was beginning to stand up, awkwardly glancing between them with an expression that conveyed a pressing desire to scarper.

'He's an old friend, Colin. We haven't seen one another in a while.' Jennifer forced a smile while her nervous system continued its frantic meltdown. She belatedly felt sorry for the poor guy standing there, looking bewildered and a little ridiculous. 'It might be a good idea if you left.'

'Are you sure, love?'

Jennifer could just *feel* Gabriel's relief. If he thought that he had won round one, then he was in for a shock, because she wasn't just going to limply cave in to whatever thin argument he brought out for them to resume their friendship and pretend it hadn't been mortally wounded.

'Sure,' she said curtly, but as soon as her date had left, she looked at Gabriel coldly.

'Satisfied?'

'No.'

'What are you doing here? I need a timeout from you, Gabriel, and I don't really care how much that's *tearing you apart*.'

'I need a drink before I have this conversation.' He paused, his dark eyes hesitant, testing the water. 'I get why you don't want to talk to me,' he said roughly. 'But I'm begging you to just hear me out.'

'Ten minutes, Gabriel, and that's it.'

'What do you want to drink? And why are you on diet cola?' He smiled, but the smile was as hesitant as his eyes had been. 'Was your date a cheapskate?'

Jennifer was having none of his attempt to introduce back the lazy teasing that had been so much a part of their relationship. She was still hurting too much for that.

'I'll have a glass of white wine. Small.'

He nodded. As he headed off, she watched him, helplessly driven to stare as her heart twisted inside her. There could be only one reason why he had shown up out of the blue. To try and get their friendship back on an even footing. To erase what had happened between them so that the clock could be turned back and they could somehow retrieve the innocent relationship they had once shared.

He'd tried to get in touch with her, but she'd ignored all his phone calls and text messages. Her bruised heart hadn't been ready to pick anything back up. There were too many links between them, however, for them to remain on opposite sides of the fence forever. Sooner or later, it would make sense for them to talk, which didn't mean that talking to him now was going to further anything. All that water under the bridge would have to do a lot more flowing before she would be able to look back and see what had been lost, with a view to finding a way to reach out and rescue some of it.

She watched him weave his way back to where she was sitting, drinks in hand.

'How did you find me?' was the first thing she asked when he'd sat down, her voice still icily unwelcoming.

'My mother sent me your address. I went round and found your housemate there, and she told me where I could find you. You never let me know where you were moving. You never answered my texts. You never returned my calls. You disappeared on me.'

'I know. What did you expect?'

'You told my mother that you couldn't see a future with a man who spent all his time working, that you had found a job in London because you needed a change… that you needed a complete break in routine to find yourself.'

'I said what I had to say, and I did what I had to do.'

'What about me?'

'What *about* you?'

'You said nothing to me, Jen.'

'Oh, I said everything to you, Gabriel. I put my heart on the line for you, and don't think you can sit here and tell me that you didn't ask for that. So where's the problem resuming our friendship? I took a risk, and do you know what I learnt?' She leaned towards him, her blue eyes as icy as the wintry Arctic Ocean. 'I learnt that what you said to me then was spot-on. I deserve better than you.'

'I know what I said. I remember every word. I know I'm sitting here and that I should expect nothing from you, but…'

'But *what*?'

'The past three months have been total agony for me, Jen. I've missed you.'

'What have you missed, Gabriel?' she said impatiently and with simmering hostility. 'The friendship or the sex?'

'Both, and everything in between.'

'Well, too bad. I needed some space from you. That was why I didn't tell you my plans or what I was doing or where I was going. Can you get that? And now that you're here, I still find that I need time away from you, so as soon as we've finished our drinks, I'd really appreciate it if you left. I'll get in touch…sometime.'

'I can't do that.'

'You don't have a choice.'

'You said you loved me…'

'I don't want to talk about this right now, Gabriel.' She drained her glass and stood up, looking around for her bag and reaching for her coat.

He stood up to tower over her.

'I need to.'

'Life's not all about you, believe it or not.'

'Hear me out. Please, Jen. For the sake of…everything we shared.'

Their eyes collided. Gabriel felt dizzy, his emotions unregulated, everything inside him churning in chaos.

He swallowed and shifted uneasily, pushing his fingers through his hair while she continued to watch him in coolly polite silence.

'Well? I'm listening, and your time's running out.'

'It's too packed and noisy in here to talk.' He glanced restlessly around him, taking in the bustling tables and the dozens of people milling around by the bar.

'Suits me. I can't imagine what we have to talk about that needs a whole lot of peace and quiet.'

'You don't have to say anything to me, Jen. You just have to listen to what I have to say, hear me out. I… I spent a lifetime taking you for granted.' He leaned forward, his voice so low and husky that she had to strain to hear him. 'We were both kids when we met. I remember it like it was yesterday. I even remember what you were wearing when I sneaked up on you, a pair of jeans and a red T-shirt, and you were so focused and earnest. I pulled your hair, and you hit me. From then on, I teased you, and you fought back. It feels like that became our thing. I felt comfortable with you, so comfortable knowing that nothing would ever get past you. You always fought right back, never let me get away with anything. I never realised how much I needed that over the years, how much I needed you in my life.'

'Don't just say stuff you don't mean, Gabriel…' Jennifer whispered. 'Don't flatter me because you think that that's the way to mend this broken friendship of ours.'

'Never call it broken, Jen. I couldn't cope with that.'

'But isn't it? The bond we used to have got broken. Things were said. This is what has emerged from it. A different relationship. It was the risk we took when…'

'No!' He drained his glass and stared at her with desperate intent. 'I needed you, Jen. Always. What I didn't realise is how closely entwined need and love are. I've loved you for so long that it was just something that was part of my life. Like I said, something I took for granted. And then…'

'And then you hatched up your wonderful plan.'

Jennifer looked at him, but she was melting inside. The love she'd spent the past three months trying to stifle was slowly uncurling and coiling its way through her. She didn't want to hope, knew that she shouldn't. Still, something in those dark, dark eyes, the misery and uncertainty there…

Her heart was beating like a sledgehammer.

She wanted him to just keep talking, wanted to bask in the aching sincerity of his voice and hear things that sent her pulse racing and her devastated heart soaring. She wanted to live in this moment. If, somehow, she was misinterpreting everything, then so be it.

'You saw the pitfalls,' Gabriel said ruefully. 'I missed them all because I was a stupid, arrogant fool. I never thought about love or falling in love. I always knew that handing my heart over to anyone was never going to happen because that's what my head had decreed. When I came up with the brainy idea to stage a relationship for the sake of my mother, I really thought that everything I felt for you could be contained, but I opened a Pandora's box—and do you want to know something?' He didn't give her time to answer. 'I'm glad I did. We slept together. If I was idiot enough to actually think that I could neatly compartmentalise the most significant thing I've ever done in my entire life, then I deserved every second of heartache I've suffered since we went our separate ways.'

'Gabriel, do you mean that?'

'Every word, my darling.' He reached out to stroke the side of her face, and she weaved her fingers into his.

'I love you so much,' she breathed. 'Like I said to you, it's just always been there, waiting to find a voice.'

'As with me. I never knew I could feel what I feel for you. I thought that love and everything it entailed—opening up to someone else, being vulnerable—was the one thing I would never do. I was cocky and blind enough to figure that my intellect and past experiences were impregnable barriers to feelings that would never be allowed to surface. When you told me that you loved me, all the old ingrained habits slammed into place, and I did what I had always primed myself to do. I shut down. Immediately and with no questions asked.'

'I missed you so much, Gabriel,' she whispered in a low, driven undertone. 'I said what I said, and I knew I couldn't go back on any of it and didn't want to, but I felt that it spelt the end of our friendship, and I couldn't bear it. I came here, turned my life on its head, but I couldn't run away from my feelings and my thoughts and my love.'

'Will you marry me, Jen? For real?'

The world was exploding into a million joyful pieces.

'Honestly, Gabriel?'

'Honestly. You're my friend, my lover and everything else in between. I never, ever want to let you go.'

'I love you, my darling, so yes. Yes, yes, yes!'

And she reached across the table, cupped his head with her hand and did what she'd spent three months longing to do.

She kissed him. Kissed him with all the love in her heart knowing that yes, what had started out as friendship so many years ago was the love she'd always dreamed of.

* * * * *